PRAISE FOR A*U*

"What a beautiful novel ab‹
hearts broken and hearts men‹‹‹‹‹. ⁄ *ug‹st ‹r ‹‹rever* will forever
chime inside my own heart."

—Gayle Brandeis, author of *My Life with the Lincolns*

"In *August or Forever*, Ona Gritz has penned a beautiful novel
about sisters. This spare, elegant story will resonate deeply
with middle grade readers in its excavation of Molly's hopes,
disappointments, and inevitable growth as she reimagines her
relationships in new ways. Exploring themes of friendship,
family, and art, Gritz deftly captures the voice of her protagonist as this tender story unfolds, defying our notions about
what it means to be a family."

—Carol Dines, author of *This Distance We Call Love* and *The
Queen's Soprano*

"*August or Forever* tenderly conveys the dynamics of a 'different' kind of sibling relationship, one between half siblings
raised thousands of miles apart. We cheer for its endearing
ten-year-old protagonist, Molly, as she navigates through un-
certainties and misunderstandings to discover that family love
has a patient, enduring force."

—Pamela Erens, author of *Matasha*

"Author Ona Gritz writes evocatively about sisters, families,
belonging, and loss in this touching middle-grade novel. Readers will enjoy following ten-year-old Molly as she witnesses the
power of art and navigates the challenges of shifting families
and friendships during an August she'll remember forever. A
story that begs to be discussed and celebrated."

—Kimberly Kenna, author of *Artemis Sparke and the Sound
Seekers Brigade*

"*August or Forever* is a tender, graceful novel about sisterhood, friendship, and love. Ten-year-old Molly is a narrator in whom young readers will surely see themselves, with her longings, foibles, and authentic voice. Sweet rather than sentimental, spare but fully drawn, this book is sure to be treasured and read again."

　—Caren Lissner, author of *Carrie Pilby*

"*August or Forever* explores the complexity of sibling relationships. Ten-year-old Molly is a believable narrator whose longing to be closer to her older half-sister, Alison, rings true. As she learns to share her parents—and her bedroom—during an extended summer visit with Alison, Molly's voice remains charming despite her flaws. Filled with a cast of well-drawn characters and settings, Gritz's novel is an insightful read."

　—Laura Shovan, author of *Takedown* and, with Saadia Faruqi, *A Place at the Table*

"In *August or Forever*, Ona Gritz introduces the relatable and artistic Molly, an 'almost only lonely,' who has long idolized her older half-sister, Alison, from afar. She is thrilled to learn that they will get to spend an entire month together when Alison flies over from England, and has the perfect plan to get her to stay forever, but reality can hardly live up to Molly's exceedingly high expectations. Misbehavior and misunderstandings threaten to ruin her summer, but the bonds of sisterhood are not so easily broken. Through characters that readers will quickly grow to love, Gritz delivers a warm and tender celebration of friendship and family."

　—Suzanne Kamata, author of *Indigo Girl* and *Pop Flies, Robo-pets and Other Disasters*

AUGUST OR FOREVER

*For Carol
with love and
gratitude for
your friendship
and the kindness
you've shown
me and this
little book.
— Ona*

Ona Gritz

Fitzroy Books

Published by Fitzroy Books
An imprint of
Regal House Publishing, LLC
Raleigh, NC 27605
All rights reserved

https://fitzroybooks.com
Printed in the United States of America

ISBN -13 (paperback): 9781646033072
ISBN -13 (epub): 9781646033089
Library of Congress Control Number: 2022935690
Lexile Score: 730L

Cover images and design © by C. B. Royal

 Regal House Publishing, LLC
https://regalhousepublishing.com

The following is a work of fiction created by the author. All names, individuals, characters, places, items, brands, events, etc. were either the product of the author or were used fictitiously. Any name, place, event, person, brand, or item, current or past, is entirely coincidental.

Printed in the United States of America

To every sister who is missing a sister.

1

Some people think that if you live in a small town like mine in Upstate New York, everyone around knows everything there is to know about you.

I'm a good example that this isn't actually true.

A lot of my neighbors, and even some of my classmates, assume I'm an only child. But I have a sister, Alison. Unfortunately, she lives really far away. *Across the pond*, she'd say.

Alison is my dad's daughter from a long time ago, when he was married to a woman named Patricia. My parents and I stay in touch with Alison through video chats, emails, and letters. Of course the video chats are the closest thing to being together. I get to see Alison up close, hear her voice, and steal little peeks at the rooms in her house. But, since there's a five-hour time difference, and Alison's been busy at university, we don't get to do this as often as I'd like. The next best is writing—snail mail style—notes and cards that arrive at our doors like surprise gifts.

We like to see each other's handwriting, and send one another drawings. Alison's are much better than mine. That's not surprising since she just spent three years studying to be an artist. Still, according to Alison, I draw better than she did when she was ten, so who knows? Maybe I'll be an artist someday too.

I have every one of my sister's notes and drawings hidden away in the chest where I keep my winter clothes. Not that Alison's a secret. I sometimes wish I could wear a T-shirt around town that says, *Actually I Do Have a Sister*. Soon, though, everyone who knows me will also know Alison. I'm not supposed to have heard this yet, but she's coming to live with us and be a regular part of our family.

Sometimes when I write to my sister, I tuck a clover or a helicopter seed in the envelope. She says she loves when I send pieces of nature. Late in May, before our lilacs turned brown and left for the year, I picked a bunch and hung them upside down on the clothesline so they'd dry and keep their color. It took two weeks for them to get papery and perfect. Then I sent them to Alison as a graduation present.

"They're brilliant," she tells me now, shifting her laptop so I get a good view of the purple bouquet in a vase on her desk.

"I'm glad you like them," I say, and I am, but I sent them nearly a month ago, and they're not exactly what I want to talk about right now. I want her to tell me the big surprise so I can stop pretending I didn't overhear my parents' conversation and figure it out.

Say it! I want to shout. *Tell me you're moving here and we'll finally get to live together like every other pair of sisters in the world.*

"What else did you get for graduation?" I ask instead.

"You already know I got to spend a fortnight at the beach in Camber Sands with my mates. That's why I didn't thank you sooner for the gorgeous lilacs."

Enough with the lilacs! I'm ready to burst. "Anything else?"

"Actually, yes." Alison pauses to grin at me. I grin back at her, aware that our smiles look really similar. Mom says it's those matching smiles that make it obvious we're sisters. Dad claims it's the eyes. Of course we don't look exactly alike. Alison is prettier. But I see something in her that feels like a part of me. It's there in her eyes, like Dad says, but it's not the eyes themselves. It's behind them, somewhere under the skin.

"Well?" I say. "What did you get?"

Alison's smile grows wider. This is it. She's about to fill me in on the best possible news.

"Dad and your mum sent me a gift that's really for both of us."

She holds up a computer printout filled with words too small for me to read, but I can make out a picture of an airplane in the corner. Even though I've known for days, my heart starts to bang in my chest. As close as we are, Alison and I have only been together once in person, half my life ago, when I was five and she was fifteen. My parents and I visited her in London for what turned out to be the happiest week of my whole life. I had a big sister to follow around and talk to whenever I wanted. Now I'll always be that happy.

"Is that...?" I say, trying to sound like I'm just putting it together now. "Are you...?"

Once again Alison gives me a grin that mirrors my own. "That's right, sis. I'm coming to see you for the whole month of August."

"August," I echo, feeling stunned.

The screen goes blurry and, for a moment, I think there's something wrong with the internet connection. But then Alison says, "Oh, sis. I knew you'd be surprised, but I didn't mean to make you cry."

"August," I repeat, wiping my eyes with the back of my hand. A month-long visit. I know it's a lot, four times longer than my stay in London all those years ago. And August is soon, just days away.

Still, it's all wrong. Alison was supposed to stay forever.

2

At dinner, Mom and Dad want to know all about my talk with Alison.

"How did she tell you?" Mom asks.

"You must have been so surprised," Dad adds.

"I was," I say, which is definitely true. It surprised me to learn Alison would be leaving us after only four weeks.

I pick up my burger and bite into it. When I glance at my parents, their faces are flushed, and they're both aiming smiles right at me, which just makes me feel guilty. They're so pleased with their gift to Alison and me, and I know I should be happy. A month-long visit with my sister is a wonderful surprise. I'd be thrilled if I hadn't gotten it into my stupid head that she was coming to stay.

Mom and Dad start planning out the details. Where Alison will sleep. What extra foods we should have in the house while she's here. I tune them out and try to remember what made me so sure Alison was finally going to live with us. My best friend Diane was over that day, the two of us stretched out on lawn chairs in my backyard, chatting about our summer plans. I was thinking of going to sleep-away camp for the last two weeks in August. My dad and I had even started filling out the online application, but I kept changing my mind. Part of me really wanted the experience. The Camp Skylark website has pictures of kids eating together, floating in row boats, talking to each other from their bunk beds. I thought being there would be a little like having a bunch of sisters, brothers, and cousins for two weeks. At the same time, I felt nervous about it. Except for the nights I've spent at Diane's house, I've never really been away from home.

What if all the other kids were friends already, and nobody liked me?

Diane and I can talk about anything, and we almost always agree, but she didn't get why I wanted to go to Camp Skylark. It's understandable. She has three older brothers and a younger sister, so her house is already like a summer camp. Meanwhile, my parents, who are both librarians, sit around every evening and read. I like books, too, but our house can be really boring with me being the only kid. The funny thing is, Diane thinks it's the best place in the world because of all the peace and quiet.

"Just do what you always do," she said that afternoon. "Come to my house when you need to be around a bunch of noise and craziness."

At some point, I went inside to get glasses of lemonade for us. That's when I heard my parents talking behind the partly closed door of the study. Mom mentioned Alison's name, which caught my attention.

"I think Alison is going to love it here," she said.

Alison? Here? I stepped closer so I wouldn't miss a single word.

"Yup," Dad answered. "When I suggested it, she practically hugged me through the computer screen."

"Molly will be thrilled," Mom added. Then she paused. "Oh, what about Camp Skylark? Can you get your money back?"

"I haven't paid. As of yesterday, she still wasn't sure she wanted to go."

"Meant to be," Mom said, and they both laughed. It's always been a playful argument between them. Mom really believes things happen because they're *meant to*, like God or nature planned it all along. Dad says that life is just full of coincidences, and it doesn't mean anything. Mostly I agree with Mom. One thing I know for certain is that sisters are meant to live together.

Still, looking back, nothing about that conversation promised anything of the kind. Then I remember something else Mom said.

"Molly has lived like an only child for so long. She's going to be so happy."

Yeah, happy for a month, I think now. After that, it's back to being a lonely only child. No, what I am is worse than being an only child. Only children don't have someone in particular to miss.

"So, Noodle," Dad says. *Noodle* was the first word I said as a baby. Unfortunately, it's been Dad's nickname for me ever since. "I've got some news about Mrs. Lamb."

Dad is the librarian at my school, so he always finds things out before any of us kids.

"What?"

"You're not going to like it," he says, and my stomach clenches up. Did something bad happen to my art teacher? She has a limp and walks pretty slowly. I hope she didn't get hit by a car or anything. Dad sighs and picks up the water pitcher to refill his cup. "She decided at the last minute to take a job in another school district."

Mom's brow crinkles up. "She's only been there a year. The kids love her. Right, Molly?"

"I know I do."

Until we had Mrs. Lamb, I didn't even realize how much I liked art. She showed us collages by an artist named Matisse, and then had us make our own. When we finished those, she brought in a slideshow of self-portraits by painters like Frida Kahlo and Vincent Van Gogh. Our assignment was to draw pictures of ourselves that didn't just show what we looked like, but revealed something about our personalities.

By then, thanks to her, art was my favorite subject. So, for my self-portrait, I drew a girl in front of an easel, drawing a portrait of herself. You see her from behind, which worked out well since I haven't gotten the hang of faces yet. Mrs.

Lamb really liked it. She also promised that, this coming year, we'd work more on faces.

"It would have been so much easier if she'd said something before summer vacation," Dad gripes. "Now we have to rush to fill the position."

"We?" Mom and I both ask.

"I'm heading the search committee," Dad says, which shouldn't surprise us. Technically, he has summers off like I do, but he's always involved in some committee or another, so he's at school all the time.

I think back to when I told Mrs. Lamb that my sister was studying art in college.

"Talent must run in the family," she'd said.

"I'm going to miss her," I tell Dad. "You better find someone good."

Then it hits me. During our video chat, before she started gushing about the lilacs, Alison mentioned that she'll have to start looking for a job now that she's finished school.

What could possibly be a better job for an artist than art teacher? *My* art teacher!

Alison can live with us after all. It's just like Mom says. Meant to be.

3

After dinner, Mom and Dad curl up on opposite ends of the couch, like they do every night, and read their books. I'm tempted to tell them my idea, but Alison should be the first to hear it. She'll be so excited.

I clear the table and wash the dishes, my one official chore. Finally, I head into the study, turn on the webcam, and scroll to my sister's number.

"Come on, come on," I say to the screen, but Alison doesn't appear. I try to remember if she said she was going out when we spoke earlier. Then I realize that it's really late in London now, after midnight.

To distract myself, I pull out Dad's album of Alison pictures. He used to keep his old snapshots from Alison's childhood in a shoebox in his closet, while the more recent photos stayed in a folder on his computer. But for his last birthday, I emptied the box and printed out the digital pictures and put them all together in this book.

I curl up on the couch and browse through it until I come to a photo of Alison when she was just a few years older than I am now, sitting with a friend on a window seat. They're squeezed close together with their arms around each other and they're grinning like they have a special secret between them, the kind of secret you'd share with someone you see all the time. I know I shouldn't be jealous. After all, I have tons of pictures of Diane and me sitting together just like that. But I can't help it. I've always been envious of the people who get to spend time with my sister. The friends who pose with her in birthday party pictures. The cousins from her mother's side, who are there for all the holidays.

I even feel jealous of Alison's mother.

Of course, I'm glad Patricia isn't married to Dad anymore. If she was, he couldn't have met Mom, and I wouldn't even be here. But why did she have to take Alison and move so far away? Patricia is British, and Dad says she went back to London after the divorce because she wanted to be near her family. Besides her parents, she has a sister she's really close to.

Well, now it's my turn to have my sister with me. I flip to the back of the album, to the one picture I have of the two of us together. Five-year-old me perched on fifteen-year-old Alison's lap.

I remember that her hair smelled like melon, and her legs were slightly scratchy under mine because she'd shaved them. Also, she was wearing her necklace with the big glass heart.

"That's pretty," I'd told Alison, taking the pendant into my hand so I could move closer to her. The glass shone with all the colors in the room.

"It's from my friend Laurel," she'd said.

For most of our trip, we'd stayed at a bed-and-breakfast. But on our last night, we stayed at Patricia and Alison's house because it was nearer to the airport.

While Alison was in the shower, I wandered around her room, trying to memorize everything. I stood at her dresser and started opening bottles and smelling stuff. Her heart necklace was in a little wooden dish, along with a pair of seashell earrings. I took it out and put it on.

"This is from my friend Laurel," I told myself in the mirror. It was fun pretending to be Alison. I opened a bottle of perfume and dabbed some behind my ears. "Lovely," I said, trying to sound as British as I could.

I sat on Alison's bed and ran my fingers along her quilt. It had a nubby feel that I liked. Her pillow had the same melon smell as her hair.

I don't remember falling asleep, but the next thing I knew,

Mom was sitting on Alison's bed, patting my shoulder. "We're running late, Mol," she told me.

I'd slept on top of Alison's covers and I was still in my clothes. "Is it morning?" I asked, sitting up.

Mom nodded. "We've got to get ourselves to the airport."

Dad appeared in the doorway with our rolling suitcases. "At least she's dressed already," he said.

Then, somehow, we were all outside. Mom and Dad were putting our bags in the back of a taxi. I remember Patricia called the trunk a *boot*, which made me laugh, even though I was still pretty sleepy.

When Alison hugged me, I noticed she didn't have her heart necklace on. What I didn't realize was that I did.

We were on the plane, buckling our seatbelts, when I discovered I had it. I quickly tucked it inside my shirt so no one would see. The heart tapped against where I imagined my own heart must be. I felt kind of guilty, but at the same time, I liked having a secret. A secret that connected me to my sister.

All through that long plane ride, I kept fingering the necklace, imagining how, at home, I'd put it on, alone in my room, and pretend to be Alison. At some point, Mom looked up from the book she was reading and noticed.

"Did Alison give that to you?" she asked.

I wanted to lie and say that she had, but I couldn't do it.

"Nah, I just borrowed it and forgot to give it back."

Mom let me keep it on for the rest of the plane ride, but when we got home, she took it from me so she could bring it to the post office the next day to send back to Alison. It's funny, but after all this time, I still think about that necklace. Alison wears it once in a while, and whenever I see it during one of our video chats, I remember how it felt, heavy and cool against my skin. I also remember how, as we flew all those miles away from London, it made me feel as though my sister was still somehow with me.

4

The next morning, the first thing I do is turn on the webcam and try to reach Alison. Again, she doesn't answer. I figure I better tell Dad my idea before they find someone else to be the art teacher. But when I look in the kitchen, Mom is in there alone, sipping a cup of tea and reading something on her e-reader.

"Where's Dad?" I ask, pouring myself a bowl of cornflakes and joining her at the table.

She glances up and tells me exactly what I don't want to hear. "He's at school, meeting with the search committee."

I swallow a spoonful of cereal. It tastes like lumpy paste. "So how long does it usually take to fill a job like Mrs. Lamb's?"

"It depends," Mom says, closing the cover on her e-reader and finally giving me her attention. "It can be harder in summer because a lot of people go away. Also, most teachers are committed to jobs already."

After hearing that, I'm hungry again. I finish the cereal, then reach into the fruit bowl and grab a peach. Meanwhile, Mom has gone back to reading.

"So," I say. "You want to hear a great idea?"

Mom looks up at me, then checks her watch. "I'd love to, Mol, but I'm already late. 'Time and tide wait for no man.'" She does that a lot, quotes from books while she's talking to you. "Why don't you head to the Kellers'?"

Mrs. Keller, Diane's mom, keeps an eye on me when both my parents are at work. It's been that way since I was a baby. These days, I'm old enough to walk over myself, but Dad always picks me up in the evenings, and we stroll in the woods before dinner. It's our private ritual.

After Mom leaves, I try to reach Alison one more time. She still doesn't answer, but I'm not too worried about it. As Mom said, most teachers have jobs already.

In our town, people hardly ever lock their doors if they're home. When I get to Diane's, I wipe my feet on the mat that says Welcome to Our Messy House and let myself in. Mrs. Keller is sorting laundry in the living room. Pete and Glen are there, too, pelting each other with balled-up socks.

"Guys!" Their mom pretends to be mad. "I thought you were supposed to be helping me."

"Can't, Mom," Pete says, ducking a pair of argyles. "Pre-season snowball fight."

She shakes her head, laughing. A ball of sweat socks lands at my feet. I pick it up and hand it to Mrs. Keller.

"Oh hi, sweetie," she says, noticing me for the first time. "Diane's upstairs."

As I head up to Diane's room, another pair of socks smacks me on the shoulder.

"Sorry, Mol," Glen calls out.

"He was aiming for your head," Pete adds.

There's a torn piece of notebook paper taped to Diane's door: *Please knock. Or better yet, please leave me alone.*

I open the door and slip in. "What's with the sign?" I ask.

Diane clicks the remote to turn off her TV, and I plop down next to her on the bed. "The sign's for Carly," she tells me. "She's driving me crazy."

Carly is only five and can't read yet. Also, this is her room too. But I don't bother Diane with those details. "Crazy, how?"

Diane grabs my hand. "She's been following me every-where, Molly. She repeats what I say. I can't even wear my overall shorts anymore, because whenever I do, she runs and puts hers on."

Carly has always done things like that, but this is the first time Diane has ever complained to me about it.

"So she copies you a bit. It's a compliment."

"A bit? It's like she doesn't have her own life. I'm all she talks about. 'Diane said this. Diane said that. Diane and I are going to do this together.'"

"I still think it's flattering," I tell her, but I'm getting a knotty feeling in my stomach. Is that what I sound like when I talk about Alison?

5

Dad rubs some spices on a chicken and puts it in the oven. Then we go for our walk while it bakes. As always, we head toward the woods in back of our house. Our special talking place. Ours and the cicadas. I can hear them chatting in the trees.

Dad takes a deep breath and stretches his long arms toward the sky. Like me, he loves the smell of pine.

On the way back from Diane's house, I made up my mind to have Dad tell Alison about the teaching job and invite her to live with us. I'm afraid if it came from me, I'd sound all *follow-you-everywhere* like Carly.

"So how'd the meeting go?" I ask, to get the conversation started. "Did you come up with any ideas for Mrs. Lamb's replacement?"

The truth is, I'm surprised he hasn't thought of Alison himself. His daughter is an artist. She babysits for one of her professors, so she has experience working with kids. And she's coming here just in time. It all seems so obvious, but somehow it hasn't occurred to him.

"No. All we did today was write up a job description and email it to the newspaper."

"Oh." I pick up a stone and toss it toward the trees. Part of me wants to blurt out my idea, but parents never listen to kids when it comes to grown-up things like jobs. I decide to just start talking about Alison. Maybe then he'll put it together.

"What was Alison like when she was little?"

"She was little."

"Really, Dad. Tell me about her."

"Alison was little," Dad insists. "She was only four when her mom and I split up."

Mom told me Dad and Patricia had what's called *a friendly divorce*. That's when both people decide not to stay married to each other, but without a lot of yelling and being angry.

"You must remember some things."

Dad sighs. "I remember she liked pickles."

"Was she anything like me?" I ask. *As in good in art*, I'm tempted to add, but I wait. I want the conversation to seem natural.

"You, Noodle? You wouldn't eat anything green until your sixth birthday. Vegephobia, I think it's called."

"I'm too old to be called Noodle!" I say for what must be the thousandth time.

I wish I'd said a normal first word like *Mama* or *Da-da*. Then everyone would have forgotten about it. "What was Alison's first word?"

"I don't know. Maybe it was *pickles*."

"Dad! Why can't you give me one real answer?"

He picks up a fallen branch that's blocking our path and leans on it like a walking stick. Something changes in his face, and I know the next time he speaks, he'll finally be serious.

"I wish I could tell you more about Alison. But that's back when I had my law practice. I was so busy in those days. Patricia was really the one who took care of her."

"Still, you were there. I'm sure you remember stuff."

"Not much. Unfortunately, my mind was more on my career than my family."

I have a hard time imagining Dad back in his lawyer years. He gave up his practice and went to library school long before I was born. He still loves to work, which is why he heads so many committees, but he's almost always home before dinner to spend time with me.

"Well, these days, you're a great dad," I tell him.

"I learned something from all I missed out on the first time around."

Dad puts an arm around me, and we walk quietly for a while. I can't help feeling kind of bad for Alison. It must have been hard having a dad who was always working. And even harder to move so far away from him.

She has to come live here. Not just for me, but for her. She deserves to have Dad the way he is now. Someone who puts family really high on his list.

"Hey, Dad?" So much for waiting for him to catch on. "Don't you think it's perfect timing for Alison to be coming? I mean, with Mrs. Lamb—"

"Anytime is perfect timing," he says, talking over me, so he doesn't hear the part about Mrs. Lamb. "But you know what, Noodle? I'm a little nervous."

That surprises me. "You are?"

"I just want everything to go smoothly. You know what I mean?"

"Yeah, I do," I say, thinking back to Diane's complaints about Carly.

We reach a clearing, and even though it's still light, we can see the moon. It looks like it's made of smoke. Like you could take a deep breath and just blow it away.

"Dad?" I hear myself ask. "Do you think Alison will like me?"

6

Before I can say anything more about Alison taking Mrs. Lamb's job, Dad realizes he forgot about the chicken in the oven and rushes ahead.

"Sorry, Noodle," he calls over his shoulder. "But we don't want flaming bird for dinner."

I take my time walking home, listening to the sound of leaves rustling overhead and breathing in the scent of pine. In my mind, I replay Dad's answer to my question.

"Alison loves you," he'd said, standing still and staring into my eyes. "You know that."

It's true. I do know Alison loves me. But maybe it's easy to love someone you don't spend much time with. You haven't seen their habits or noticed their faults, so they don't get on your nerves. Besides, whether Alison loves me wasn't really what I'd asked. I'm her sister, so she pretty much has to love me. What I don't know yet is how much she'll *like* me once she's here every day. It occurs to me that I may have been thinking of things in the wrong order. Alison has to love being here. She has to want to stay. Otherwise, the best job in the world could come up, and it wouldn't really matter. I'm not sure how I'll do it, but I have to show Alison how much we're missing out on by living apart. Then, when she tells me she wishes that she could afford to stay, I'll say, *Actually, I happen to know of a great job that will make that possible.*

By the time I get home, Mom's there too, and before I know it, we're sitting down to eat.

"Guess who has a new book out?" Mom asks Dad, which means she's been reading reviews and ordering books all day. She's the head of our town library, and every month, on ordering day, she and Dad have this exact conversation. They go on and on, all through dinner, about their favorite authors and what new novels they want to read.

Usually, once I'm done with my kitchen chores, I head up to my room and draw for a while. But tonight, I'm not in the mood, so I lounge in the study and watch old sitcoms on *Vintage TV*. It seems every show from when my mom and dad were growing up was about a houseful of kids. Big brothers play tricks on little sisters. A pair of twins gets in trouble at school when one tries to take a test for the other. A boy runs away from home and camps out in the playground until his sisters figure out where to find him.

Finally, I turn off the set and pull out the Alison album again. I also take down another album that's filled with pictures of me from the time I was a baby. For a while, I compare my photos with Alison's, focusing on whether we look alike at various ages. Then I try to match the years. The fact that she's exactly ten years older makes it easy to do the math. My first birthday and Alison's eleventh. A picture of me at seven and one of her at seventeen. If we grew up in the same house, like those TV families—actually like every family I know—all these pictures would be combined in one album. We'd also have a ton of photos of Alison and me together.

I flip back and forth for a while longer, and then I get an idea. One that just might plant the thought in Alison's mind that she should stay.

7

The next morning, as soon as Mom and Dad leave for work, I call Mrs. Keller and tell her not to expect me until after lunch. That gives me plenty of time to work on my project.

First, I choose all the pictures I'll need and put them in piles.

The Alison pile and the Molly pile.

And, by itself, the picture of the two of us together.

I sit at Dad's computer and start scanning and printing. It takes a long time, but finally I have two of each photo. The original to keep, and a printout for Alison's present.

I put my supplies in a box and carry that up to my room. Even though no one else is home, it's my favorite place to work on art projects.

I settle in, take ten sheets of Mom's cream-colored stationary out of the box, and fold them down the middle. Next, I sew them together with cream-colored thread.

It looks just like a real book.

Leaving the cover page blank, I open the book and tape in a picture. Alison leaning over a birthday cake shaped like a dollhouse. Underneath, I write as neatly as I can,

The year Alison was ten...

I turn the page, tape in a picture of me as a baby, and write,

...her sister Molly was born.

On the next page, Alison is sitting at her desk in a classroom. School is all mixed up and different in England. They don't even have anything called high school.

The year Alison started Grammar School...

Turn the page:

...Molly took her first steps.

Then, Alison with a wide, silvery smile:

The year Alison got her braces...

Followed by me in a head-to-toe snowsuit:

...Molly played in the snow for the first time.

Next, Alison in cutoffs, leaning on a car:

The year Alison became a teenager...

...Molly went to her first library story hour.

Then, Alison in her school play:

The year Alison played the nurse in Romeo and Juliette...

Followed by me covered in blotches of red and blue:

...Molly finger painted in preschool.

I turn the page, tape in the photo of the two of us, and write,

The year Alison was fifteen and Molly was five, they finally met.

The year Alison celebrated her sixteenth birthday...

...Molly started first grade.

The year Alison graduated grammar school...

...Molly played an apple tree in her school play.

The year Alison started university...

...Molly earned a sewing badge in Girl Scouts.

The year Alison traveled with friends to Paris...

...Molly won third prize at her school science fair.

I'm ready to end there, leaving the last page blank like I've seen in lots of real books. Then, I get a better idea. I write,

The summer Alison was twenty and Molly was ten, they were finally together again.

Above that, I trace the outline of a photo. Inside the rectangle, I write, *Place Picture Here.*

Last of all, I bring out my colored markers and write the title on the cover.

Once Alison reads *The Sister Book*, I know she'll understand. "Oh, sis," she'll say. "We have so much time to make up for."

8

As I walk to Diane's house, I'm feeling pretty good. I think *The Sister Book* is beautiful, and I'm confident Alison will think so too. More importantly, it does a great job of delivering its message.

Mrs. Keller is busy in the kitchen when I arrive, and all three of Diane's brothers are crammed in front of the blaring TV. I call out, "Hi!" but no one hears me.

Upstairs, I find Diane yelling at Carly. "Don't you ever touch my stuff again. Ever!"

"I won't," Carly answers. "And anyway, I didn't."

"Yeah right," Diane mumbles and starts tossing things around on her desk.

"You're a meany, anyway," Carly tells her and leaves the room, slamming the door behind her.

I plop down on Carly's bed. "What did she take?"

"My cherry gum."

"Gum? You're this mad because of gum?"

"It was my last piece!"

"She's only five," I point out, and as I do, I picture myself at five, fiddling with Alison's necklace on the plane. True, I didn't take it on purpose, but I would have kept it if I could have.

Diane sits down next to me and sighs. "You're probably right. A piece of gum shouldn't be that big a deal. It's more that she never leaves me alone. She's not just all over my things, she's all over me. I'm telling you, she has no life of her own."

My stomach starts to knot up like it did the last time we had this conversation. *Sisters are supposed to be close*, I want to say. Though what do I know on the subject? I've always assumed that, to be a good sister, all I had to do was love Alison and be myself. But what if my *self* turns out to be too much like Carly's?

Meanwhile, I still haven't told Diane that, at least for now, Alison only plans to stay for a month. It actually embarrasses me to say aloud that it's never even occurred to my sister or my parents that we should all live together like a regular family.

"So what do you think of Alison taking over for Mrs. Lamb?" I ask Diane for starters.

Diane grabs my hand. "That's perfect! Is she excited? She must be."

"I just came up with the idea myself. I haven't suggested it yet."

Diane drops my hand and stares at me. "Oh, Mol, you better hurry up."

"I know. But Alison will be here soon, and my mom told me it takes a long time to find new teachers, especially in summer."

"No," Diane says. "I mean you really better hurry up. Your dad called this morning and asked me to tell my mom that he might be late coming to get you this afternoon. He said he had to stay and interview someone."

9

I felt sure you were mad at me," Mom tells Dad at dinner. We're having lasagna, which is my favorite food in the world, but I'm not very hungry. Dad left work so late that he called me at Diane's and told me to come home by myself. No stroll in the woods. No chance to find out if he gave Alison's job away.

Dad shakes his head at Mom's comment. "That's too funny, Gail."

"I texted your dad to remind him about something," Mom turns to me and explains. "He wrote back, 'Am I forgetting this?' which I interpreted as, 'I didn't forget, so why are you bothering me?' I walked around all day feeling bad about it."

"Meanwhile," Dad adds, "what I actually meant was, 'I did forget. Tell me what you're talking about.'"

"'The single biggest problem in communication is the illusion that it has taken place,'" Mom quotes.

"Yup. You should have just asked me," Dad says, chuckling.

I'm not sure if the misunderstanding is funny or not. All I want is for them to stop talking long enough for me to ask Dad about the interview. Finally, I give up and just break in.

"So, Dad, did you hire a new art teacher?"

He takes a forkful of salad and chews for what feels like an hour.

"Well," he says, pausing again to sip slowly from his water glass. "We met with a woman today who might be worth considering."

"What's she like?" Mom asks.

"Very experienced," he says. "She's been a teacher up in Royerville for twelve years."

Something sinks inside me. Alison has only ever babysat and been a student.

"Sounds good," Mom says. "At this late date, maybe you should just go for it."

Dad finishes a huge mouthful of lasagna before he responds. "Maybe. But she's a second grade classroom teacher, so art is just a small part of what she does. You never know. She could be good. We're just not sure if she's creative enough and if she's capable of engaging the older kids."

"Dad, you should hire an artist," I say, giving him one more chance to figure out who the perfect person would be.

"That's definitely one way to go, Noodle. The district allows uncertified teachers two years to get the necessary coursework done while they're on the job."

Meant to be, I think, sitting up a little straighter as I wait for him to piece together what I'm suggesting.

But he just continues to eat. Finally, I can't help but explode with it.

"Dad! What about Alison?"

There. I've said it. I half expect a light bulb to appear over my dad's head and streamers to drop from the ceiling. But he looks at me blankly for a moment, then turns to Mom.

"That reminds me. Tomorrow's the retreat, so we scheduled this woman's second interview for the day after. Do you think you and Noodle can get things ready for Alison without me?"

"But, Dad, you don't need to interview that lady again. Alison—"

"Of course we can. Right, Mol?" Mom asks, giving me a look that tells me I'm arguing too much. She turns back to Dad. "Now, remind me how to inflate that darn air mattress."

Dad launches into a long set of instructions, so I just slink off to my room where I sit, turning the pages of *The Sister*

Book. This morning, when I made it, I felt sure it was perfect. But right now, it just looks babyish. Worse, I realize it kind of makes it seem like Alison is all I ever think about. Finally, I just hide the thing in my cedar chest under a bunch of sweaters.

10

When I wake up the next morning, Dad's already left for the retreat. That means he won't be reachable until tomorrow, after Alison is already here and his interview with the Royerville teacher is over.

"Can't I just give him one quick call?" I beg Mom as she stands at the stove, flipping pancakes. "I doubt they've even gotten started yet."

"Sorry, Mol," she says. "You know the rules."

Unfortunately, I do. The retreat happens every summer. The staff from my school goes to a local hotel and stays overnight to brainstorm new ideas for the coming year. For nearly two days, they're not allowed to check email and answer cell phone calls unless they're pretty sure they involve a life or death emergency. It's as if some wonderful new way to teach will fly out of their heads if anyone dares to interrupt them.

Mom puts our breakfast on the table and sits across from me. "I know. You'd think they were working on a plan for world peace."

"Tell me about it," I say, drizzling syrup over my pancakes.

She takes a sip of her tea. "Meanwhile, you and I have plenty of our own work to do if we're going to get this place ready for Alison."

I sigh and poke at my food. What could I have said to Dad in two minutes anyway? *Hire your daughter. She'd be perfect for the job. Okay, bye.*

I decide to just throw myself into helping Mom, the one person who's taken time off from work to make things nice for Alison.

We straighten up all the rooms downstairs, then I dust while Mom vacuums. When we go up to my room, I squeeze my clothes into my two top dresser drawers, so Alison can have the two on the bottom. Next, Mom and I pick up all the games, markers, and drawing pads I've left on the floor and pile them neatly on my bookcase. The books also go back on the shelves. Finally, there's room for a second bed in there.

We find the air mattress in the attic over the garage. My room may have been messy, but this place is a total disaster. It's really bright because of the skylight, so you can't help but notice how dusty it is. Plus, there are boxes everywhere. Most are labeled—*M's Baby Clothes, Tax Stuff to be Shredded, M's Report Cards*—but some are just blank. From the looks of it, my parents never have thrown anything out in all the years they've known each other.

The air mattress starts out as a flat sheet of rubber, but after Mom inflates it, and we make it up with sheets and a summer quilt, it looks totally comfortable. We've also brought a spare lamp and a small table down from the attic, which we set beside the bed. I can't believe the transformation. It's a room for two, just like I'd always imagined.

11

The next day, I hang out with Diane in her front yard until it's time for Mom and me to pick up Alison at the bus station. I really wanted to drive to New York City so we could meet her plane, but when my mom offered to make the trip, Alison insisted she could get to our town on her own.

"The instructions are right here online," she'd said on our last video chat. "Besides, it's all part of the adventure."

A few feet away from Diane and me, Glen and Robbie toss a soccer ball around. Glen calls for us to join them, but we shake our heads. Not that we have anything better to do. We've spent the last half hour teasing ants by making an obstacle course out of twigs.

I try not to think about the fact that my dad is in some office at school right now, probably giving away the job that should be my sister's.

"So I guess Carly is still driving you crazy," I say.

Diane nods and rolls her eyes. "Wait till you see her haircut. She actually brought my picture with her to Shortcuts to show them what she wanted."

I blush. Just recently, I decided to let my chin-length hair grow out, figuring that since Alison looks good in long hair, I would too.

"Did she really?" I ask, picking up the twigs to set the ants free.

Soon, the yellow day-camp bus pulls up in front of the house. The door hisses open and Carly comes out, looking just like a mini Diane. Backpack swinging, she runs to where the boys are playing.

"Watch it, dumb-head!" Robbie hollers as he almost trips over her.

"Don't call her that," Diane yells.

Carly turns toward us and rushes over.

"Like my hair, Molly? It's the same as Diane's."

"I see that."

"My little sister's making me nuts," Diane says, but she sounds proud this time instead of angry.

Carly chats to us about her day at camp, showing us her half-finished lanyard, describing her strategy for winning at dodge ball, and giving us a detailed list of everything on the lunch menu.

While she talks on, Diane pulls Carly down onto her lap and kisses her short, spiky hair.

Now I'm really confused. Does she love her or hate her? Or is it some combination of both, that as an almost-only child, I'll never understand?

12

When Alison steps off the bus, she looks like she does in pictures and over the webcam, but different too. Prettier and less pretty at the same time.

"Molly."

Maybe it's the accent, but whenever she says my name, it sounds like a gift she's presenting to someone important. She wraps me in a tight, swaying hug.

Alison is really here. The person who's holding me right now is my sister!

"I'm so glad you're here," I tell her at the exact moment she tells me, "It's so good to see you."

We both laugh, and then Mom steps up to take a turn hugging Alison.

"Welcome, sweetheart."

I duck into the space between them and there we stay, a circle of family, breathing each other in. Alison's hair still smells like melon.

"How was your flight?" Mom asks on the drive home. "Did you have any trouble finding your way to the bus terminal?"

I'm in the seat behind Alison and, without thinking, I start stroking her hair. When I notice I'm doing it, I stop. *She's not just all over my things, she's all over me*, I remember Diane complaining. Alison must feel differently, though. She reaches back to squeeze my hand and, for the rest of the ride, holds on to it.

Before long, we turn into our driveway and let ourselves in through the back door.

"What a lovely kitchen," Alison says, glancing around.

She's right. It's big and bright, and the windows frame the prettiest trees in our yard.

"I think you'll like the whole house," I tell her. "We set up my room so it's now for both of us. Want to see?"

Before she can answer, Dad comes in, carrying a big pizza box. I study his face, trying to figure out whether he gave away the teaching job. But, of course, there's no way to know. He stands there awkwardly, like he's not sure what to do with the box he's holding. Finally, Mom takes it, and he and Alison put their arms around each other.

"Hey, Dad."

It feels strange to have Alison right here in our house, calling my father *Dad*. I definitely like it. This is having a sister. Still, I'm pleased when he reaches an arm out and includes me in the hug.

"All my girls together in one room," he says.

When we sit down to eat, Dad asks Alison all kinds of questions. About her friends and university, about Patricia, and about how London has changed since the last time we were all there.

Meanwhile, I keep sneaking peeks at Alison. I wouldn't say my sister is beautiful, but it's almost as though there's this light that shines inside her. You can see she likes herself—in a good way. I'm sure it makes other people like her too.

"Remember old Mrs. Cornwall who ran your bed-and-breakfast?" she asks Dad. "Remember the eggs?"

"Boiled or fried?" Dad barks in a pretend English accent.

Mom and Alison burst out laughing.

"I really wanted to ask for an omelet," Mom says. "But I was afraid she'd kick us out."

"What'll it be?" Dad puts his hands on his hips. "Boiled or fried?"

As I sit there listening to them talk and joke, I catch myself wishing Dad would turn to me and call me Noodle, even though I usually hate that. I guess I have back and forth feelings about my nickname, just like Diane has about Carly.

Finally, there's a pause, and Mom asks Dad how the interview went. "Would you believe we talked to that woman for over an hour, and *she* wound up telling *us* no?" he says.

I feel so relieved that I let out a little laugh. Everyone turns to me, so I explain to Alison that my art teacher unexpectedly quit. I watch her carefully, waiting for her eyes to light up. *Come on, Alison. You need a job. We have a job right here that would be perfect for you.*

"Dad heads the search committee," I put in, thinking they can start the interview right now while we finish our pizza.

"The teacher you told me about?" Alison asks. "Mrs… Lion, is it?"

"Lamb." *Art teacher. Job opening.* Maybe if I think the words loudly enough, they'll find their way into Alison's brain.

But all she says is, "Ah, sis. You must be absolutely gutted. I know you loved her."

Alison peels another slice of pizza from the box and turns to my parents. "Molly showed me the portrait she did where she's drawing herself drawing. She's got talent, this one."

"Runs in the family," I say, like Mrs. Lamb once did. For a moment, I really miss her. But Alison grins at me, and it strikes me that Mrs. Lamb's leaving the job was like a gift to us, even though she didn't know it. Even though Alison doesn't know it yet, either.

Soon, everyone goes back to reminiscing about our London trip, retelling stories I barely remember. The nice part is, Alison keeps glancing my way and smiling. And when Dad does a pretty bad imitation of a British accent, she turns to me and winks.

Mom brings out dessert, a pecan pie from the farmer's market, and while she cuts into it, Dad asks Alison, "So, have you figured out anything for the fall?"

This is it, I think, holding my breath. *He does get it. He's going to offer her the job, after all.*

"Actually, I've got good news on that front, Dad."

Alison waits while Mom passes the plates of pie around. My stomach tightens. I have a feeling this isn't good news at all.

"I've told you all about the Clarks, right?" Alison asks.

"Sure," Dad says.

Mom nods.

Roger Clark is a painter Alison studied with at university, the one whose kids she babysits for. The Clarks have two children, Stephanie who's seven and Byron who's four.

"Well, they've offered me a live-in position," she announces. "They're clearing out an upstairs room for me."

It takes me a moment to understand. "You're going to live with the Clarks?"

"Righto. I'll be a full-time nanny like Mary Poppins."

This is too much. Stephanie and Byron Clark will get to live with my sister, and I won't?

"But you're an artist," I remind her. "Being a nanny would just be a waste of your talent."

"Molly!" Mom says sharply.

"It's fine," Alison says. "That's actually a good point, sis, and if this were an ordinary nanny job, I'd have to agree with you. But it's more an apprenticeship."

I stare at her blankly.

"I'll get paid to live with the Clarks and help them with their children, but Roger Clark is also going to keep teaching me. It's an incredible opportunity, really, to work with him one on one. I'm so flattered that he agreed to take me on. My mates at school are all a bit jealous."

"Oh, Alison, it sounds terrific," Mom says, and I turn to glare at her. Terrific? It's a disaster.

Alison goes on, talking with her hands the way I've seen her do on the webcam when she gets excited. "My room will be at the top of the house, on its own floor. It has great light and plenty of space for an easel."

"'A woman must have money and a room of her own,'" Mom recites. "Virginia Woolf wrote that in 1929, and those are still the two essentials for a creative life."

Usually, it doesn't bother me when Mom throws quotes from books into a conversation, but right now it makes me want to throw some books across the room.

"To my countrywoman, Mrs. Woolf," Alison says, lifting her water glass.

My parents do the same, and they all toast her plans to leave us.

13

L ater, while Alison unpacks upstairs in my room, and my parents are lost in their books, I call Diane.

"What's the matter, Mol?" she asks as soon as she hears my voice. "Alison get there okay?"

"She's here," I sigh.

"Hey, listen, I know Alison's twenty. But that means she was a teenager just a year ago, and they can be really obnoxious sometimes for no reason."

At first, I don't understand what she's talking about. Then I realize Diane thinks Alison has been mean to me in some way.

"Alison is really nice," I say.

"Oh. So?"

I take a breath and tell her everything. That I was wrong in thinking Alison had ever planned to live with us. That, instead, she'll live with the Clarks in the perfect room with perfect light. Finally, I describe how Mom made it worse by tossing in that stupid quote from some British writer.

"What does that even mean?"

"You know," Diane says. "Artists need their own place where they can work without worrying about being interrupted."

I do know that. Even though my parents are such bookworms, I almost always draw up in my bedroom. That way, neither of them will suddenly look up from the page and say something like, *Oh, Molly, I forgot to tell you*...right when I'm really involved with what I'm doing. When that happens, it feels as though I was in the middle of a great dream, and a loud alarm clock screamed in my ear. Maybe that's why I couldn't call Dad while he was at the retreat. Maybe planning the school year can take you to that dream place the way making art can.

The one person who gets this about me is Diane, which is why she's the one person I'll let join me in my room while I draw. We'll sit next to each other on my bed, and she'll quietly work on poems. Diane loves to write, but never gets to do it at home for obvious reasons.

I guess I'd always assumed it would be the same for Alison and me. We'd sit in our shared room in the evenings, each silently working.

I think of everything Mom and I did to make my bedroom a perfect space for two. Emptying drawers, organizing my stuff, carrying the lamp and table down from the attic.

"The attic!" I blurt. "That's it!"

"What are you talking about?"

"The attic over our garage. I know it's a complete mess, but it's bright and would make a great art studio if we clean it up. Don't you think Alison would stay if we did that for her?"

"Possibly," Diane says, but she sounds doubtful.

"Why only *possibly*?"

"Well, you also said she was really excited that she'll get to keep working with her art professor."

"Alison doesn't need to be a student anymore," I tell Diane. "She's already such a good artist, it's definitely time for her to be the teacher."

14

As I head up to my room, I'm buzzing with excitement over my plans for Alison's studio. Her own family, a place to do her art, and a great job teaching what she loves. Of course she'll choose it over being Mary Poppins at the Clarks' house.

"Lovely," she says when I come in. "I was hoping you'd join me soon."

She hums as she sorts through her things. There are piles everywhere. Books. Jeans. Shoes. It's hard to imagine how it all fit in her two suitcases.

"Is there anything important in this?" She nods toward the chest where I've hidden *The Sister Book.*

"Winter stuff," I answer, sitting on the chest as though she just reminded me what a comfortable chair it makes. "Why?"

She frowns at the heap of T-shirts on the bed. "I hate that you had to crowd your clothes," she explains. "I figured I could give you back one drawer and use that."

"It's okay."

There's a soft knock on the door, and Dad peeks his head in. "Anything I can get you?" Dad asks Alison. "More pillows? A British to American dictionary?"

She laughs. "I think I've got everything, Dad. Thank you."

"Don't keep her up much longer," he tells me. "Those crazy Brits think it's one in the morning right now."

I nod.

"Good night, girls," Dad says.

"Night, Dad," we answer together. For a moment, it feels as if we've done it every night of our lives.

As soon as Dad closes the door, Alison turns to me.

"Tell me everything," she says. "Hold nothing back."

Before I can answer, she shoots a bunch of questions at me all at once.

"Favorite color? Favorite foods? What's your favorite time of day?"

I laugh. Is it possible we've never talked about any of this over the webcam? I guess we haven't, since I don't know what her answers would be.

"Blue, lasagna, and dinnertime," I tell her.

"Ah, dinnertime." Alison smiles. "I'd have to say that's a favorite of mine as well."

"Favorite food?" I ask back.

"Chocolate."

"Color?"

"Ummm. I don't think I could choose. Maybe it wasn't fair of me to ask that of a fellow artist."

I grin, thrilled to be called an artist, especially by my artist sister.

Alison puts the last of her clothes in my dresser, then lets out a noisy yawn.

"Guess I am a bit knackered," she says.

"You're what?"

Alison smiles. "We have some funny expressions across the pond. *Knackered* means *tired.*"

For a long time, I lay in the dark, listening to Alison breathe. It's a comforting sound. So this is what it's like, I think, to share a room. Of course, Diane and I share a room on our sleepovers, but this is different. My sister and I are finally doing what siblings do. We're joining our daily lives together.

The problem is, I'm not at all tired. Usually, I switch on the lamp and draw until I get sleepy. But the light might wake Alison up, so I'm stuck. The funny thing is, I feel a little annoyed about it, but at the same time, I like feeling that way. It's so normal.

Finally, I grab a drawing pad and creep downstairs. I settle on the couch in the study and let my pencil move across a clean page, sketching leaves and branches until what I have in front of me looks like one of the ancient oaks in the woods behind our house. In autumn, when the leaves turn their bright, fiery colors and start to drop, I always pick a few off the ground and mail them to Alison.

I'm in that nice dreamy mood drawing always puts me in, so it takes me a moment to realize I've just come up with another way to get my message across to Alison. The reason she's so appreciative of gifts like leaves and flowers is that she lives on a busy London Street. When we talk on the webcam, and she hears birds or crickets in the background from my open window, she always tells me how lucky I am.

"Listen," she said recently, leaning back in her desk chair. We both sat quietly, staring at each other through our computer screens. From her window, I heard car horns, sirens, and the rat-a-tat-tat of a jackhammer. Alison sighed. Clearly, she's tired of living in a big, noisy city. And as it happens, the Clarks live in noisy London too.

First thing tomorrow, I'll take Alison for a walk in our woods. Really, they belong to just Dad and me, our private talking place, but I'm sure he'll understand.

"Alison?" I say when I wake the next morning.

Turning over, I see that her bed is an empty rumple of blankets and sheets. She's probably downstairs having breakfast.

I putter around the room, getting used to how it looks with Alison's and my things mixed together. Her hairbrush next to my comb on the nightstand. The clothes we each wore last night draped on my rocking chair. Her necklaces and bracelets dangling from the doorknob with mine.

I check to see if the necklace with the glass heart is there, and sure enough it is. Carefully, I lift it away from the others and hold it in my palm. The heart is not as heavy as I remember, but it's just as pretty, mirroring the light and picking up colors from around the room.

The catch is tricky. You have to unscrew one half from the other to get it open. For a moment, I wonder how I ever did it when I was small, but I realize the necklace was big enough on me then to fit over my head without my having to unclasp it.

I get the chain open and, as I do, one side slips from my hand. Before I can stop it, the heart pendant slides off the dangling end and lands hard on the floor.

"Oh no," I cry, watching it shatter.

15

I pull on socks so I don't cut my feet on the glass, then pick up the largest shards and toss them in the wastebasket. There's still a glittering layer of dust-sized pieces, so I grab a wet washcloth from the bathroom to wipe them up. Finally, I get dressed and, tucking Alison's empty chain in my pocket, head downstairs with the trash bag.

Thankfully, no one's in the kitchen, so I can shove the bag into the bin under the sink without having to answer any questions. I drop into a chair and lay my head on my arms. In my mind, I hear Diane yelling at Carly, *Don't you ever touch my stuff again. Ever!*

Glancing around, I notice cereal bowls in the sink and spilled oatmeal on the counter. Dad and Alison are probably running errands in town. At dinner last night, they'd talked about getting some kind of card that will make her cell phone work here in America.

I gulp down a drinkable yogurt, then go out to wait on the back steps. This way, I can stop Alison from heading inside and noticing what's missing before I have a chance to tell her.

To my surprise, Dad's car is parked in the driveway. Before I can figure out where they might be, I hear Alison calling to me. "Good morning, sis!"

Dad comes out behind her, through the break in the trees that leads to our woods.

"You went to the woods?" I stare at Dad.

He grins. "How else am I going to show off to my sophisticated city girl?"

It's like he stole my idea. But how could he do that if I never even said it out loud?

"It's so beautiful back there," Alison gushes. "You can really hear your own thoughts."

"Didn't you say you had to go to the cell phone store?" I ask Dad. I know I shouldn't feel mad at him for taking Alison to *our* place, especially since that's exactly what I planned to do. Still, I can't help how it bothers me.

"Been there and back, sleepyhead," he says.

I wish I'd been sleeping. Then Alison's heart necklace would still be hanging on the doorknob, all in one piece.

"Well, girls," Dad says. "Off to work for me."

"You're going in? Now?" What can he possibly have to do at school that's more important than being here with us on Alison's first day?

"I'm afraid I don't have a choice, Noodle. We've got several people to interview this week."

"For Mrs. Lamb's job?"

I glance at Alison. She's staring at the sky, watching a hawk glide overhead, as though this has nothing to do with her.

"Yup," Dad answers, sounding pleased. "We're getting good responses to our ad. I think we'll be able to fill the position pretty quickly."

Now that she's already seen the woods, I ask Alison if she wants to go meet Diane.

"Your best mate? I'd love to."

The Kellers are our closest neighbors, but it still takes about ten minutes to walk from our house to theirs. On the way, I know I should tell Alison about the necklace, but I can't seem to get the words out. In fact, I can barely get any words out at all.

"Am I remembering right that you and Diane have been friends since you were in playpens together?" Alison asks.

"Yeah."

"I've had two of my best mates since I was four or five. Since we first moved to England."

"Oh."

"This would be a lovely spot for a bicycle ride. At home, I ride almost everywhere."

"Yeah?"

Alison probably can't believe what a boring blob I've become. It's like I've turned into that blank on the last page of *The Sister Book.* Place Personality Here.

When we get to Diane's house, she and Carly are sitting on the front porch in their old-fashioned swing that's hung up on chains.

"Look who's here!" Carly yells. "Hi, Molly. Is that your sister?"

I introduce everyone to each other, then sit sideways on the top step so Alison can have the one deck chair.

"Before we heard you were coming," Diane tells her, "Molly was planning to go away to camp at the end of August. So that's one reason I'm happy you're here. I don't know what I'd do for two whole weeks without her."

"Is that true, sis?" Alison asks. "You missed out on summer camp for my visit?"

"I go to camp," Carly announces, climbing onto Diane's lap. I remember sitting on Alison's lap like that, her heart necklace cool against my back. The thought of it makes me mad at myself all over again.

"So what do you like to do at camp?" Alison asks Carly.

The screen door bangs open, and Robbie rushes out. He stops when he sees my sister.

"You're the one from England," he tells her.

Brilliant, Robbie, I think. *Like she didn't already know.*

"That's me!" Alison says.

And to my surprise, she grins at him.

Wherever Robbie was going couldn't have been too important. He stands between Alison's chair and the steps, blocking her view of me. I can still see her, though. She stretches her arms over her head, which makes her shirt creep up. I notice for the first time that she has an earring in her belly button. Robbie stares at it. "What part of England are you from?" he asks the earring.

As Alison answers Robbie's questions, I'd swear her accent gets thicker. That didn't happen last night when she and my parents were talking about London. I get the feeling she hopes Robbie likes her, and not just as a friend.

It never occurred to me that Alison might want to date someone. If it had, the last guy I would pick for her is Robbie Keller. He's the oldest of Diane's brothers, so they're closest in age, but he's definitely not the nicest.

As the two of them yammer on, Carly gets bored and goes inside, freeing Diane to join me on the step. As soon as she does, Robbie and Alison both decide to sit on the swing.

"Isn't this perfect?" Diane whispers in my ear.

I stare at her. "Perfect, how?"

She checks to make sure Alison and Robbie are still only paying attention to each other, which, of course, they are.

"If they become boyfriend and girlfriend, she's definitely not going anywhere."

16

Of course, Diane is right. A boyfriend could be just the thing to make my sister want to stay. I'm actually proof that such things happen.

Before my parents met, my dad lived with some friends in a mountain town an hour away from here. He came down for a weekend conference for librarians at Mom's library, and they happened to sit next to each other during one of the workshops. Afterward, they went out to lunch. They must have had a great time. Dad was supposed to go home two days later, but he never left.

I guess I should be glad that Robbie and Alison are hitting it off. The problem is, I don't trust Robbie at all. Meanwhile, Diane keeps watching the two of them like they're starring in some great romantic movie. Clearly, she's forgotten about what she and I call The Baseball Incident.

The Baseball Incident happened last spring when Diane and I decided it might be fun to try out for the softball team at school. Neither of us had any experience, so we invited a couple of friends from our class to practice in the clearing one Saturday.

Because she has so many brothers, Diane had enough mitts for all of us. She brought them out, along with a couple of baseballs she found lying around their room. We had a four-way catch, and soon discovered that each of us was terrible in a different way. Diane couldn't catch, and when I threw, the ball most often landed behind me. Our friend, Bridget, couldn't help ducking whenever she saw the ball coming, and our other friend, Lila, threw high and far, but she had horrible aim. We lost both balls in the woods within the first hour.

"Maybe softball tryouts aren't such a good idea," Diane said after our other friends had gone home.

Since we'd all played equally badly, we'd laughed a lot and had a good time. We were still joking about it when we got back to Diane's house, which was how Robbie heard the story.

"Wait," he'd said. "You lost two of our balls in the woods?" He ran upstairs and, a moment later, came bounding down. He was furious.

"My Yankee ball is gone," he screamed at Diane.

She stared at him and grew really pale.

"I can't believe you let that happen," he yelled, shoving her so that she almost fell backward. "You better go find it, you little pain."

Knowing Diane as well as I do, I could tell she was trying hard not to cry. When we were alone on our walk back to the woods, she let it out.

"He caught that ball at a Yankee game," she explained to me between sobs. "Some big hero of his hit the winning home run, and everyone in the stands wanted that ball. But Robbie was the one who got it."

The two of us hunted for hours, searching behind every tree, and climbing as high as we could to check the branches. Now and then, Diane had to stop to cry again.

"I'm the worst sister in the world," she wailed.

"No, you're not," I tried to assure her. "It's not like you lost it on purpose."

When the sky grew dark, we headed back, agreeing to meet after dinner with flashlights. But almost as soon as I got home, the phone rang.

It was Diane. "After all that, it wasn't even his Yankee ball," she told me.

"You're kidding. Why did he think it was?"

Diane sighed. "He didn't. He knew all along that his precious Yankee ball was safely tucked away in his sock drawer."

"Then why…"

"Supposedly to teach me a lesson. He figured if he made me feel bad enough about it, I'd stop treating his stuff like communal property."

I couldn't believe it. "But that's just mean. We spent all that time—"

"I know."

I thought of a scarf I once had with a pattern of dark red roses. It was made of a light, sheer material, and the first time I wore it, a strong wind came and blew it right off me. The scarf fluttered into the street in front of my school and was immediately run over by a van. It lay there squashed, the colors dulled by the grime from the road. That's how Diane sounded on the phone right then. Flattened. All her brightness gone.

"Just be glad you don't have brothers," she said.

"What kind of music you into?" Robbie asks Alison now.

She names some bands I've never heard of, but Robbie seems to know them. He tells her he's thinking of going to see a group called X-Ray Vision in New York on Friday, and asks if she'd like to come.

Alison's eyes brighten. "A concert in New York City? I'd love that."

Diane elbows me. "While they're on their date," she whispers, "we can get to work on the attic."

17

The countryside here is beautiful," Alison says on the way home. "It reminds me a bit of Lancashire. But yours is a lighter green. I suppose that's because you get less rain."

The last thing I want to talk to my sister about is the weather. I consider describing The Baseball Incident as a warning against Robbie. But if I'm going to bring up little sisters taking things that don't belong to them, I should confess about the necklace and I'm not quite ready to do that.

I sigh. What I'd really like right now is to be by myself for a few minutes. It's so strange. All I've wanted for so long is to have my sister with me. I guess I'm just used to taking a moment here and there each day when I can be alone with my thoughts. It calms me.

But then, so does being in the woods, and I suppose there's no reason Alison can't go twice in one day.

"Brilliant," she says when I suggest it.

We walk to the clearing where Alison and I stretch out in the grass and listen to the birds. Meanwhile, I try to think of ways to talk to Alison about staying.

"So, umm, you know how Dad works at my school?"

"Yeah." Alison faces me and props her head up on her hand. "What's that like? Does he treat you differently from his other students?"

I flash back to an afternoon last year when he slipped and called me Noodle in front of my classmates. For about a week afterward, kids kept calling me Spaghetti-Head. That was one time I wasn't thrilled to have Dad at school, but I don't tell Alison this.

"Of course it's great when families get to spend time with each other," I say.

Alison nods and I study her face, waiting for her to realize that she can be with us too.

"Well, now that my art teacher left..."

"Yeah, I've been thinking about that, sis."

"You have?" My heart revs. Maybe she is considering the job!

"There's such freedom in your drawings," Alison tells me. "That's something you want to hold onto, no matter who your next teacher is."

I nod and try to focus on what she's saying, even though it's not what I'd hoped.

"We artists can get really caught up worrying about what others will think of our work before we even finish it," she goes on. "To me, the trick is letting go of all that and recalling how to play, like a child. If you remember to do your art because you find it fun, you'll be ahead of a lot of people."

I think of *The Sister Book*. Part of why I didn't want to give it to Alison was that I thought she'd find it babyish. But if I understand what she's saying, she'll see that as a good thing.

"Do you mind waiting while I run back to the house and grab something?"

As I rush home through the trees, it feels as though the birds on their branches are cheering me on.

Up in my room, I take *The Sister Book* out of the chest and shove it in my backpack before I can change my mind. By the time I'm back in the clearing, I'm sure it'll work its magic and show Alison why she should stay.

Kicking off my shoes, I plop down beside my sister. "So, I made something for you."

Taking a deep breath, I pull *The Sister Book* out and hand it over. *This is it, Alison*, I think. *This is how it's supposed to be for us.*

At first she just gazes at the cover, then she sits up and carefully begins turning the pages. Alison takes her time studying each picture. I imagine it's coming to her slowly, the realization that, of course, families need to live under one roof. Her mother had that with her all this time, and now it's our turn. I let myself picture Alison and me walking to school together in the mornings and bumping into each other in the hallways between classes. *That cool, new art teacher is really your sister?* kids will ask, and I'll beam with pride.

Finally, she reaches the end and closes the book. When she looks up at me, her eyes are all misty. She gets it.

"Molly, this is just lovely."

"You really think so?"

Alison nods. I wait for her to say more, but she goes back to the book, reading it through a second time.

"You were so adorable," she tells me, pausing at the photo of me at three. "Oh, and look at me here with those awful braces on my teeth. I hope you never have to go through that."

With a jolt, I realize that she sees *The Sister Book* as a cleverly put-together photo album. She likes it, but she doesn't get what it says.

"So, anyway, I meant it to show what it would have been like if we'd grown up together."

Alison stops browsing through the photos and looks up at me.

"We missed out on a lot," she finally says. "Didn't we, sis?"

"We sure did." For a moment, I think I might start crying.

Alison runs her fingers through the grass. I know she's wishing that there was a way she could stay. I'm bursting to suggest she take Mrs. Lamb's old job, but I wait. I want it to come together perfectly.

"Are those sparkles on your socks?" she asks me suddenly.

"What?"

I glance down and realize there are bits of glass stuck on my socks. Alison picks at one and studies it. It's too tiny for her to recognize where it came from, but I decide it's time to tell her what happened. If we're finally going to live together as sisters, I don't want anything to ever come between us. No secrets. No lies.

I reach into my pocket and pull out the empty chain. Alison stares at it.

"Where did you get that?" she asks, taking it from me.

"I'm really sorry," I say. "I was just trying it on and—"

She cuts me off. "Where's the heart?"

"I'm sorry," I tell her again. "It fell and broke."

Alison stands up and shoves the chain into her jeans pocket. Without a word, she starts walking toward the house, leaving *The Sister Book* in the grass. I pick it up and follow her.

"It was just glass," I call out. "Not diamonds or anything." Too late, I realize I've said the exact wrong thing.

She spins around and glares at me. "It was a gift. The one thing I had from a mate I'll never get to see again. You ever loose a mate, Molly?"

I shake my head, though I feel like I'm losing one right now. "Did she move away?"

A single tear runs down Alison's cheek.

"Laurel died," she tells me.

18

When we get home, Alison goes straight upstairs and closes herself off in my room. I'm not sure what I should do.

Mom and Dad are both home from work. I can hear them opening cabinets and clanking pots in the kitchen. For a moment, I wonder what happened with Dad and the interviews, but then I realize it doesn't matter anymore. Alison is never going to want to live here now.

Meanwhile, I'm still holding *The Sister Book*. What am I supposed to do with it? Just a little while ago, Alison said it was lovely. Now, I'm sure she hates it like she hates me.

I go into the study, sit at Dad's desk, and stare at the computer screen. It's dark and blank, just like my mind.

My sister's friend died. She died. And I went and broke the one keepsake she had from her.

I imagine Alison is stretched out on her bed, facing the wall the way I do when I'm upset. Like her, I always shut the door behind me, though what I really want is for one of my parents to knock and come in. Eventually, one of them always does. Even if it's the person I'm mad at, the company makes me feel better.

So, though I'm nervous, I grab *The Sister Book*, head upstairs, and knock on my own door.

"Alison? It's me. Can I come in?"

When I don't hear an answer, I poke my head in. Alison is lying on the air mattress, wearing ear buds and staring at the ceiling. She's holding the chain from the heart necklace and running her fingers along the links. But when she turns and sees me, she puddles it in her fist like she wants to hide it.

Her eyes are puffy and red the way mine get when I've been crying. Seeing her like that makes me want to cry too.

"I'm really sorry," I say.

"Don't worry about it," she tells me. "It was just glass, like you said."

But I can tell she doesn't mean it. Her voice is like my old smashed scarf.

"Alison, I—"

"I'm just really knackered," she says, turning away. "Can you please close the door behind you?"

I place *The Sister Book* on top of some other books she's left on my dresser and do as she asks.

19

Y ou're not, by any chance, a fan of roller coasters, are you?" Dad asks Alison that night at dinner.

"No, Dad. Not Lessing's Cove," I plead.

"Oh, come on, Noodle," he says, mussing my hair.

Lessing's Cove is a small family-run place that's more like a permanent country fair than an actual amusement park. But they have a few monster-sized rides, which is why it's the last place I want to go. Anything that zooms, spins, flies, or turns upside down makes me feel nauseous and miserable.

To my dad, the bigger and wilder the roller coaster, the better. Fortunately for him, my mom doesn't mind rides like that. And fortunately for me, Diane feels the way I do.

Last year, when we were nine, Mom gave me her cell phone and let us walk around Lessing's Cove by ourselves while she and Dad went on the rides we don't like. Diane and I rode the merry-go-round a couple of times, then spent the rest of the day talking and eating junk food.

"I think roller coasters are smashing," Alison tells Dad.

Judging by Dad's grin, I'm pretty sure that means she likes them as much as he does. "What do you say, Noodle? Ready to give it a try?"

Alison is looking down at her plate. Clearly she's still mad at me.

I shrug. "Maybe just the two of you should go, since I'm such a ride-wimp."

"I'll be at work all day," Mom reminds me. "Invite Diane. You'll have a good time."

Dad pokes me in the ribs. "Cotton candy's on me."

"Do you mean candy floss?" Alison asks.

She and my parents start comparing American and British words for things. After a while, I leave the table to call Diane.

"My dad wants us to go to Lessing's Cove, but I'd rather just hang out at your house." From where I'm sitting in the living room, I can see Alison wander into the study. She chooses a book from the shelves, kicks off her shoes, and stretches out on the couch. I figure she plans to read until she falls asleep, and then just stay there the rest of the night. That's what I would do if I didn't want to be with me.

"Let's go to Lessing's," Diane says. "We haven't gone in forever."

"There's a reason for that," I remind her.

"Come on, Mol," she pleads. "You and I always have fun, no matter where we are."

I really want to tell her about the necklace and Laurel, but I hear Carly and their brothers horsing around in the background, so I know now is not the time for that conversation. Maybe if we go to Lessing's Cove, we can talk while Dad and Alison ride the roller coaster and the other terrifying rides.

"All right, let's do it." Through the doorway, I see Alison turn a page in her book. The fact that one of her good friends died is almost too sad to think about.

For a moment, I try to imagine how I'd feel if Diane ever died. I'm sure I'd never be happy again.

When Diane climbs into the backseat beside me the next morning, Carly scrambles in after her.

"Hi, Molly. Hi, Alison. Hi, Mr. Rhodes," she says.

Somehow Diane hears my question without me having to say it.

"No camp today," she whispers, pressing her forehead against mine. "I was only allowed to come if I brought her with me."

As we turn off their quiet street onto the main road, I stare out the window, hoping to hide my disappointment. It's not that I don't like spending time with Carly. I really do. But I was counting on talking to Diane in private.

One thing I'd tell her is how, today at breakfast, Alison and I avoided looking at each other. Meanwhile, she and Dad talked easily. Just like they're doing now, as though the rest of us aren't sitting right here behind them.

Out the window, I catch sight of a billboard advertising Lessing's Cove. In the picture, a crowd of people manages to scream and smile at the same time from the top of the roller coaster.

"Something For Everyone at Lessing's Cove," the thing says in big letters.

The next billboard for Lessing's shows a woman and a girl sitting on the merry-go-round together. It's hard to tell whether the woman is supposed to be a very young mother or a much older sister. I think of the blank space I'd put at the end of *The Sister Book*, the one that's meant to hold a photo like that of Alison and me.

While Alison was in the bathroom this morning, I noticed that she left *The Sister Book* on my dresser exactly where I'd put it. Not only that, she'd thrown a couple more books on top like she wanted to bury it.

"Molly?" Carly says, leaning against me. "Isn't it great that we all get to go to Lessing's Cove together?"

"Are you sure you guys don't want to give the roller coaster a chance?" Dad asks Diane and me as soon as we're inside the park. He has to yell to be heard over the ride's thundery rumble and the roar of everyone on it screaming in unison.

"No way," I shout, expecting Diane to echo me.

But she looks up at that huge, twisting, metal torture device like she's actually considering it. "Maybe we should try it just once. Maybe our tastes have changed since last year."

I can't believe it. "Diane! You get dizzy and sick just like me."

"Really, I was just scared. Let's try."

Dad squeezes her shoulder. "Atta girl. What do you say, Noodle?"

What I want to say is that my best friend is a traitor. Instead, I remind him that someone has to stay behind with Carly.

"I'll keep an eye on the sprog," Alison offers.

It's the closest she's come to speaking to me all morning, but I can't help thinking she's said it just to bug me.

"No, I'll watch her," I say, glaring at Diane.

I expect Dad to tell me I'm too young to be responsible for Carly by myself in a big park like this. But he points to a nearby bench and orders us to stay put. Then he takes off with the others.

20

All around Carly and me, people laugh and chat and hug each other as they walk.

On the bench next to ours, a bunch of teenagers tear off tufts of sky blue cotton candy and toss them into each other's mouths. Most of the time, they miss, but that just seems to add to the fun they're having.

Two girls who look like sisters stroll past us, holding hands and singing "Frère Jacques." They remind me of Diane and me. They also make me think of how I wish things were between me and Alison.

I'm almost ready to cry when Carly points to a man wearing a round clown nose and big clown shoes, which is especially strange since, other than that, he has on regular clothes. We watch him take a balloon out of his pocket, blow it up, and twist it into the shape of a little dog. A moment later, he sneaks up behind us and places it on Carly's head.

"Thanks, Mr. Clown Man," she calls after him.

This isn't all bad, I tell myself. Soon, Diane will join us. We'll put Carly on her favorite ride, small motorcycles that move in a slow circle, and then I'll finally get to talk to Diane about what a mess I've made of everything.

From where we're sitting, we can see the roller coaster and hear constant bursts of screaming. Everyone on it yells and lifts their arms as they whisk down from the very top, just like on the billboard. I catch sight of Dad and Alison as they do it, blocking Diane from my view. I'm sure she's hating every minute of whipping up and whizzing down on that thing.

"Don't be surprised if your sister feels sick when she comes down," I warn Carly.

"We'll be good nurses for her," she tells me.

When the crashing sound of the roller coaster finally stops, I crane my neck and watch for three familiar faces, figuring they might be among the last we'll see, since Dad and Alison probably have to hold Diane up and help her walk straight.

"There they are!" Carly calls out, pointing into the crowd. After a moment, I spot them. Either Diane is acting brave just for show, or I'm seeing wrong. She, Dad, and Alison stroll arm in arm, laughing and talking.

When Diane sees us, she breaks free and runs over.

"Molly, it was great! You have to try it," she says.

All I can do is stare at her. "You're not dizzy and nauseous?"

"I'm a little dizzy, but not in a bad way. I can't wait to go again."

"That's what I like to hear," Dad says, having made his way over with Alison. "What do you say, Noodle? Ready to brave this thing?"

"Wasn't that fun?" Diane asks Alison.

"Righto," my sister says. "I could do this all day."

I stare up at the roller coaster and try to picture myself in one of the seats that's hurtling down from the top. If I could make myself do it, would Alison forgive me?

"I . . ." I want to say yes, but the thought alone makes me feel sick to my stomach. "I'll take Carly over to the kiddie rides."

"You sure?" Dad asks.

"Sure."

Don't let me, I'm thinking. *I'm only ten*. But I can't say it out loud. When I want him to give me independence like this, I use the same argument. *I'm not a baby, Dad. I'm ten*. Maybe I've said it too many times.

He tears off a string of tickets and hands them to me. "We'll meet over at the concession stand at one, okay?"

Watching them walk off, I notice what a nice family the three of them make.

I turn to Carly. "So. What do you want to go on first?"

"Wait," she says. "Your daddy's coming."

It's like a scene from a movie, the way Dad rushes back through the crowd. When he reaches us, he's out of breath. As soon as he's able to speak, I'm sure he'll tell me he's changed his mind and plans to keep me company while Carly goes on the little rides.

It will be nice to have some time together, Noodle, he'll say.

But then I see Alison and Diane standing still and watching, like they're waiting for him.

Dad pulls his cell phone out of his pocket and places it in my palm.

"Call or text Alison's number if you need anything."

21

I never knew it was possible to ride in a car with four other people and feel completely alone. But that's where I am, and that's how I feel. As Dad, Alison, and Diane all talk about what a great day they had, I stare out the window and wish I were in any one of the other cars zooming by. Even Carly is chatting away, telling the others about the new ride where we sat in a teacup as it went around in drifty figure eights.

"Then Molly and I bought a big bag of caramel corn and ate the whole thing."

Even when I hear my name, I don't feel as though I belong. It's like they're the family and I'm the babysitter they brought along.

"Thanks for staying with her," Diane whispers, making me feel a little better.

She loops her arm through mine, then yawns and lays her head on my shoulder.

Diane and I have known each other for so long, I can't even remember when we first met. Once, I asked her if she recalled meeting me.

"We were born friends," she'd answered.

Now her breathing slows, and I realize she's fallen asleep. Part of me wants to shake her off and pick a fight after the way she abandoned me today. But the truth is, I love the feel of my best friend resting against me.

I can't help but think again about how sad I'd be if she ever died. If there was no Diane, I'd probably feel so heartbroken, I'd never want to leave my room. Meanwhile, Alison is laughing with Dad in the front seat like her friend Laurel never existed.

Maybe my sister and Laurel weren't really that close. After all, Alison only had that one necklace from her supposed mate. I have a roomful of things Diane has either given me, or left at my house like it was just part of her own.

I have Diane's red umbrella, a bunch of her stray barrettes, her Rubik's Cube, her gel bracelet that says *Girl Power*. There's the jewelry box she gave me for my birthday. The backpack she let me keep when I told her I liked it. It's almost like *we're* sisters. I know for sure she feels closer to me than to her awful brother Robbie.

I wonder if Alison would still want to date him if she knew about The Baseball Incident. Who knows? Maybe she'd think it was a perfectly good way to teach his little sister not to take his things without asking.

The next thought that enters my mind startles me so much, I must actually jump because Diane wakes up and stares at me.

What if Laurel—if there *is* a Laurel—didn't really die? What if Alison made it up just to teach me a lesson?

When we get home, I head straight to my room and close the door. Let Alison be the one who feels like she has to knock this time.

"Alison lied about Laurel." I say it out loud to try and hear if it seems true. Teenagers don't go and die for no reason. But would Alison just make that up so I'd feel worse about breaking the necklace? It's exactly what Robbie did with the baseball. No, it's much worse. What kind of person *kills off* a friend just to make someone else feel guilty?

I dress for bed and then lie in the dark, listening to my family's voices drift up from the kitchen. Alison has a loud laugh, and every time I hear it, I feel like it confirms my theory. That's not the sound of someone who's lived through a real tragedy.

After what feels like a long time, the door creaks open, and Alison quietly changes in the dark. To my surprise, she whispers my name. Maybe she's ready to try and make up. It's a little late for that, I want to tell her. Instead, I pretend I'm sleeping.

22

In the morning, I take my time going down for breakfast. When I finally do, I find Alison and my mom leaning together over Mom's laptop, clicking through pictures on some fashion website.

"That's cute," I hear Mom tell Alison as I pull the juice out of the fridge.

"I don't know, Gail," Alison says. "It's a bit posh for what I have in mind."

"Molly!" Mom sings like she's just noticed me. "I'm playing hooky so I can take Alison to the mall to pick out an outfit for tomorrow. Wanna come?"

"What's tomorrow?" I ask, sitting at the table with my bowl of cereal. I know it's Alison's date with Robbie, but I can't help wanting her to think I don't care enough to remember.

"It's my day in New York City," Alison says.

Her day. A whole day. I thought they were just going in for a concert at night. Why do I care? I shouldn't care. She and Robbie deserve each other.

"Come with us, sis." Alison touches my arm. "I can use your opinion."

She really is ready to forgive me. Or at least she's ready to stop punishing me. But now that I'm pretty sure she lied about Laurel, I'm not ready to forgive her.

"No thanks," I say. "I was just at the mall like a week ago."

I thought Alison and Mom would leave right after breakfast, but they don't seem to be in any hurry. While Mom catches up on email in the kitchen, Alison closes herself off in my room as though it's her own. I think of how happy that would have made me a day ago, back when I was sure I wanted nothing more than for her to make this her home.

For a while, I slouch on the couch in the study and flip through TV channels. I feel more like drawing, but of course my pad is closed off in my room with Alison.

If I could, I'd head to Diane's, but I know she's on her way to the orthodontist. I'd almost rather be the one about to have metal cemented to my teeth than be me right now.

Finally, I pound up the stairs to my room. Let Alison find somewhere else to hang out. But as I reach for the knob, she opens the door and nearly bumps into me.

"I'm just taking the rubbish down," she says, blushing. She has my wastebasket in her hand, which had been empty since I threw out the broken glass. Now, it's filled to the top with crumpled papers.

"That stuff goes outside in recycling," I tell her.

From my room, I hear her go out the back door and come back in.

"There you are," Mom says. "We should get going."

"I'm ready," Alison tells her.

"Mol?" Mom calls out. "You sure you don't want to come?"

"I'm sure," I yell down.

After they leave, I glance around my room for my drawing pad. That's when I notice Alison's pile of books has gotten shorter. The thing that's missing is *The Sister Book*.

I look on the nightstand, on the floor by the bed, and underneath the air mattress. I dig through the drawers I gave Alison for her clothes. I even check her empty suitcases.

From outside, I hear a familiar rumble. It's the recycling truck, just in time to swallow those torn-up pages with their carefully chosen photos.

23

Tears drip into my ears as I lie on my back in the clearing. As much as I love being in the woods, right now it just reminds me of the last time I was here, when I gave Alison *The Sister Book*.

I should have known then that she'd throw it out. She hadn't had it for five minutes before she abandoned it in the grass. If I hadn't picked it up, it would still be here, the pages growing stiff from the sun and wet from dew. I saved it, or so I thought. If I'd left it here, *The Sister Book* would still exist.

I'm just taking the rubbish down, Alison had said, turning red because I'd caught her.

The confusing thing is, she seemed to be trying to make things better between us. Did she destroy my gift because I wasn't so easy to win over?

When I'm all cried out, I get up and walk to Diane's. I could let myself in, but I don't feel like being around her noisy brothers. I sit on the porch swing and wait. For the first time in what seems like forever, I think about Camp Skylark. If I had signed up, I'd be leaving in a few days. I'd get to swim, paddle a canoe, make new friends, and tell stories around a campfire. Instead, I'm stuck here with my awful sister.

Finally, the Kellers' minivan pulls into the driveway. Carly runs out first.

"Diane got braces," she says, plopping next to me. "I wish I could get some, too, but my teeth are still babies."

Diane and her mom come up the steps after her.

"Can I stay here tonight?" I ask.

I'm anxious to fill Diane in on all that's happened, but her teeth really hurt, so we curl up together on the couch and watch a couple of our favorite movies to take her mind off the pain.

"I'm show gad you're here," she mumble-slurs.

"So am I," I say, and try to let the movies make me feel better too.

"How's your mouth?" I ask Diane in the morning. I'm lying across the room from her in her sister's bed. Whenever I sleep over, Carly stays in their mom's room.

"It doesn't hurt as much," Diane says, sounding like herself again.

I pick up one of Carly's baby dolls. She's got eyes that open and shut when you tilt her head back and forth and a fake-looking, painted-on smile.

"Diane? Can I talk to you about something?"

Before I even start, hot tears stream down my face. Diane grabs a tissue box and sits beside me while I finally tell her everything.

"Well," she says when I finish, "I know with my brothers, if you think they're lying, they probably are."

"I figured that with Robbie. But Pete and Glen too?"

"Yeah, usually. Did Alison say how Laurel died?"

"No. She got so upset, we never talked about it."

"Sounds like Alison made it up, but maybe not on purpose."

I stare at her. "How can someone lie by accident?"

Diane shrugs. "I could see it. She felt really angry that you broke her necklace, but part of her knew she shouldn't be making such a big deal out of it. So, she came up with a story to match her reaction."

It shouldn't make sense, but somehow it does. Once, I spilled a bowl of chicken soup and burst into tears. "We'll just clean it up," my mom said. "It's nothing to cry over." I didn't really know why I was crying, which made me feel embarrassed, so I told Mom the soup burned me.

Holding up Carly's doll, I have it ask Diane, "How come you're so smart?"

Her cheeks turn pink. "I'm not. It's just that I've exaggerated like that too."

"Still, telling me her friend died was going pretty far."

"Maybe it just came out of her mouth, and she didn't know how to take it back."

Outside Diane's closed door, the Kellers' house is coming alive. I hear the guys racing down the stairs and Carly talking to their mom in her high voice. It occurs to me that you probably learn a lot by living with so many people.

"Okay. So maybe Alison didn't mean to lie about Laurel. But she still threw out the book I made for her."

Diane picks up the doll and rubs its bald head. "Are you totally sure she did?"

"It was there the night before, and then, yesterday, she brought a bunch of crumpled paper down to recycling. And she turned red when she saw me see her. After that, the book was gone. I looked everywhere."

As I describe all this, I'm really hoping Diane thinks I'm wrong and will come up with a better explanation for what happened to *The Sister Book*.

But she shakes her head. "That is mean. If she didn't want it, she could have just given it back to you."

24

While Diane and I eat breakfast—a fruit smoothie for her sore teeth and toaster waffles for me—we re-watch one of last night's movies.

"Haven't you seen this like a million times?" Robbie asks, joining us on the couch. He has on clean black jeans and, for the first time ever, he smells like cologne.

Diane glances over and notices his nice outfit. "Who are you, and what have you done with my brother?"

"So," I say, keeping my eyes on the screen. "Going to the city soon?"

Robbie snatches a waffle off my plate and bites into it. "Yup. I'm leaving to pick up your sister in a minute."

"I thought the concert wasn't until tonight."

"It's not, but I thought we'd walk around the Village and go into the old record shops and stuff." He stops as though he just remembered who he's talking to. "Why? Do I need your permission?"

As soon as Robbie leaves, Diane turns to me. "Let's go work on the attic."

"Should we?" I ask. "I don't even know if I want Alison to stay after August."

"Well, you might change your mind. And anyway, we have nothing better to do."

I sigh, still unsure that it's worth the effort.

"Hey," Diane says, pulling me up off the couch. "Look at it this way. If you decide not to give it to Alison as an art studio, I could use a quiet place to go now and then."

When we reach my house, we spot Robbie and Alison standing in the driveway. Alison's wearing a new gauzy blouse

and white pants, and her hair is in a loose braid. I guess she
did fine at the mall without me.

We wait until they climb into Robbie's car and drive off
before we head to the garage and up to the attic.

"Why don't you clear off those shelves?" Diane suggests.
"Then we can put some of these boxes up there."

The shelves she points to are covered with all kinds of
odds and ends. Torn greasy T-shirts of my dad's, rusty old
pliers, a wrench stuck in an open position, scattered nails. At
first, I feel overwhelmed as I try to think of where to put
everything, but then I realize I can throw most of it away.
Dad has all new tools hanging up in the garage, and plenty
of clean shirts. I find an empty trash bag and fill it with everything but the nails. Those I scoop into a jar I find lying
around, which I'll take down to the garage and place with
Dad's newer tools.

Diane brought a tub of cleaning wipes from her house,
so I pull one out and wipe down the shelves, then turn to
see what she's working on. I find her sitting cross-legged on
the dirty floor, looking through the baby book my mom put
together when I was first born. It's got photos of me in the
hospital, still attached to my mom by a blue umbilical cord,
and others where I'm wrapped in a receiving blanket and
wearing a little cap on my head. Mom taped in the official
certificate with my inky footprints, the baby announcement
she and Dad sent out to friends, even the little hospital ankle
bracelet that says, Baby Girl Rhodes.

"Diane, we'll never get done if you stop to read through
everything," I complain.

But when she looks up at me, I see her cheeks are wet. I
stop what I'm doing and sit beside her.

"What's the matter?" I ask, putting an arm around her. I
wish I could give her a tissue, but all we have up here are the
cleaning wipes.

"Your parents saved all these things." She points to the

marked boxes waiting to go up on the shelves. "Your homework from every year, your report cards, your old clothes."

"I know it's a lot, but we'll get through it."

Diane wipes at a tear with the back of her hand. "It's not
that I mind the work. I'm jealous. Look at all the time they
took with this book. My mom didn't make anything like this
when I was born. I guess she couldn't, since she had three
other kids running around. But still. She's never even put our
photos in an album. They're just shoved into a desk drawer."

I'm so surprised that I don't know what to say. Diane
jealous of me?

"Yeah, but we hardly ever look at this stuff."

"Even so. Doesn't it tell you how special you are to them
that they keep it?"

"But, Diane, they keep everything," I point out, pulling
the broken wrench out of the trash bag and holding it up.

Diane laughs, and I hug her, glad I can make her feel a
little better.

"And anyway," I add, "I've been jealous of you my whole
life."

"No way! Why?"

"Isn't it obvious? Your family all lives together."

"Not my dad," Diane says.

It's true. Mr. Keller hasn't lived with them since before
Carly was born. In fact, they hardly ever hear from him.

"Sorry, I didn't think of that. I guess I kind of forgot
about him."

"Says the girl with the nicest dad in the world."

"He is pretty nice. But you still get to live with all your
siblings."

Diane nods and wipes her eyes. "Well, let's get this room
fixed up and maybe you can too."

"Yeah, maybe," I say, but I'm still not sure it's what I really
want anymore.

I head down to the garage and grab Dad's radio to make

the cleaning go faster. As we work, we sing along to songs we like and imitate the goofy commercials. After everything is up on shelves, and the trash is thrown away, I sweep and mop the floor.

"Hey, Cinderella," Diane calls. "Look what I just found."

She pulls what looks like a bunch of wooden rods out from behind her back.

"What is that?"

Grinning, she unfolds it and stands it up under the skylight.

I can't believe it. An easel. Maybe Alison really is meant to stay.

25

The art studio looks so inviting, Diane and I decide to hang out there a while. Earlier, we'd found cushions from my parents' old couch and set them against the wall as comfy places to sit. As we lounge on them now, she works on a poem. I do my best to sketch her, but I'm still not very good at faces.

After Diane goes home, I head up to my room and lie down. My muscles are really sore from all the lifting and cleaning. Still, it isn't long before I feel restless and find myself poking around through Alison's things. Just like in London, I open her bottles of perfume and sniff them. I leave the jewelry on the doorknob alone. At least I've learned that lesson.

Her books are still stacked on my dresser. I pick up each one, hoping *The Sister Book* will appear, but of course it doesn't. When I come to a sketchbook, I know I should leave it in the pile. After all, snooping through Alison's stuff started our trouble in the first place. Then again, I can't exactly break anything by looking through her drawings.

The book is filled with portraits, and they're all really good. The faces are shaded just enough to create natural looking shadows and angles. I recognize Alison's mom Patricia and a few cousins from photos we have. I turn to a drawing of an older couple, probably Alison's British grandparents, and one of Alison's aunt who looks like a chubbier Patricia. After that, there's a bunch of self-portraits. In them, Alison looks like herself, only younger. She puts the date on each drawing, so I know this book is from three years ago. I wonder why she didn't bring any newer sketchbooks with her.

After the drawings of Alison, I come to page after page of people I don't know. My mind starts to drift, and I realize I should call Dad to tell him I'm already home so he doesn't go looking for me at Diane's.

He picks up quickly. "Hey, Noodle. You're home early. Listen, I just finished the last interview of the day, but we still have to debrief. Dinner's going to be on the late side, okay?"

The interviews! How could I have forgotten? "So, um, did you find someone to hire?"

Dad sighs loudly. "I wish I had better news, but no. The first guy was a no show. Then we interviewed a woman who's so overqualified, I'm sure she'd leave within the year if a university job came up. And the last one actually didn't sound like he likes kids very much."

"So what about Alison, Dad?" I blurt, even though I have such mixed feelings about her right now. Maybe this, like the easel, is a sign that Alison is meant to live here and teach at my school.

But, as usual, Dad misses my point entirely. "She'll be out late tonight," he says. "It'll just be the three of us for dinner."

Next, he goes into a speech about not opening the door to strangers or letting anyone online know I'm here alone.

"Yup. Uh-huh," I say, and start flipping through Alison's sketchbook again. When I get to the last page, I find a portrait of a teenage girl, kind of floating in the sky. "I'll be careful," I promise Dad and quickly hang up the phone.

Underneath the floating girl is a field with a single headstone.

"Laurel Jane Manning. Beloved daughter, granddaughter, sister, and friend. Rest in Peace," it says in letters that appear to really be carved in the stone.

I study the birth and death dates below the inscription. They're fourteen years apart.

Laurel died one year before my parents and I visited Alison in London.

She was four years older than I am now.

Here's something else about that picture. On the grass, in one corner, is a shiny glass heart.

And something else about Laurel Jane Manning: she looks familiar.

26

I stand the sketchbook by Dad's computer and pull the photo album I made for him down from the shelf, letting myself imagine for just a moment that I'll find *The Sister Book* tucked in the bookcase behind it. Of course, it's not there. It's nowhere.

Sinking into Dad's desk chair, I flip to the window seat picture, then place the album beside Alison's drawing. The girl sitting next to Alison in the photo has Laurel's round cheeks, her dimpled chin, and curly hair. A shiver slides through me.

I remember the way I used to stare and stare at this photo, wishing away Alison's friend so I could take her place beside my sister.

All this time, I was jealous of a dead girl.

Carefully, I peel the picture off the page and turn it over. The date, in Alison's loopy handwriting, is just two months earlier than the date on the headstone in her sketch. How could I think Alison would lie about something so heartbreaking?

Resting my head in my hand, I feel the butterfly-shaped barrette I clipped on this morning. I'd helped myself to it from a tray on Diane's dresser without even thinking. Now, I tug it out of my hair and stare at it. How would I feel if Diane died and this was the only thing I had that belonged to her? Even though it's nothing special or expensive, I know I'd cherish it the way Alison cherished the necklace I'd stolen from her twice. I'm terrible at being a sister. No wonder Alison got rid of *The Sister Book*. She probably wishes she could get rid of me.

I squeeze Diane's barrette so hard it digs into my palm. Finally, I start to cry.

I wish Dad were here. The last time he and I sat here together, we looked at pictures of Camp Skylark. Back then, my biggest problem was deciding whether to brave a two-week adventure away from home, or have the slow, easygoing kind of summer I was used to.

Camp Skylark. I want to snap my fingers and be there right now. Even if I didn't make one friend, it would be better than staying here, ruining my relationship with my sister.

Wiping my eyes, I tap Dad's mouse to wake up his computer. I go online and see that he still has the camp website marked as a favorite. Soon, I'm clicking through photos of kids drifting on a lake in rowboats, hiking in pairs down a shaded trail, splashing off a dock and laughing. "This place looks fun," I remember Dad saying. He joked that he'd like to go with me.

Suddenly, a message pops up on the screen: IT'S NOT TOO LATE TO COMPLETE YOUR RESISTRATION FOR OUR AUGUST II SESSION! it says in big, bright letters.

"It's not?" I ask aloud.

I click on the link and my registration form comes up.

It's all still there, completely filled out. My address. My birthday. The answers to a long list of medical questions. Dad's email and cell number. Mom's. Even Mrs. Keller's, since she's my emergency contact.

At the bottom of the page is a button that says: *Pay Now*. If I click it, am I done? Am I registered for camp? That would give Alison two weeks to make a decision about staying, without me here messing things up. In fact, she'd understand that my leaving was a gift to her. A much better gift than *The Sister Book*.

Pay Now. My heart bangs in my chest, but I click on the button, squeezing my eyes shut as I do.

When I open them again, I see pictures of credit cards and the question, *How would you like to pay?*

Well, I guess that's that. Alison is stuck with me. I have no idea what credit cards my parents have, or how to go about using one.

Below the links for Mastercard and Visa, I notice something called Pay-Buddy.

Do you want to go to your Pay-Buddy account? it asks.

I click *Yes*, only because it sounds so friendly.

On the Pay-Buddy page, the user name is already filled in. *BookBen.* My dad. The only thing missing is the password.

What would he use?

I try our last name. Our phone number. The name of our street. Mom's name, *Gail. Alison. Molly.*

I'm about to give up, but then I think of one more possible word.

Noodle, I type, and a new page opens.

Welcome to Pay-Buddy, it says. *Click here to confirm your payment to Camp Skylark.*

27

I have my hand on the mouse, my finger ready to press down and make it official, when I hear the front door bang open.

"Molly? We're home," Mom calls.

"Great," I mutter.

"Mol? We brought take-out." Her voice is coming closer, so I quickly click off the Internet, afraid that if I hurry with the payment, I'll wind up doing something wrong, like paying twice.

No matter. I know the form is there. I know the password. All I have to do is get through dinner, do my kitchen chores, and wait for my parents to settle in with their books.

"There you are," Mom says, leaning in the doorway. "Did you have a nice time at Diane's?"

"It was okay." I grab Alison's sketchbook and excuse myself.

Up in my room, I sneak one last look at the drawing of Laurel and her grave before placing the book back in the pile. My throat closes up and I'm afraid I might cry again. I can't believe she had just two months to live when she sat smiling next to Alison in the photo. I also can't believe I ever doubted my sister.

Taking a breath, I nod to myself in the dresser mirror. "I have a plan," I say aloud, which makes me feel a little better.

In the dining room, Dad is unloading takeout boxes onto the table, while Mom pours cups of tea for us.

"Chinese, huh? From the Fortune Palace? Did you get me sesame chicken?" I'm trying to sound normal, but realize I'm talking really fast.

"Yeah, about that." Dad gives me a teasing grin. "We almost did, but then I thought you might want to try something new. So we got you fried octopus with a side of turkey intestines."

"Do turkeys even have intestines?" I find the chicken and start filling my plate.

"Sure do. Here they are." He pokes his chopsticks in a box and pulls out a clump of rice noodles. "Crispy. Yum."

It's not until I start eating that I realize how hungry I am. Now that I've figured out what to do, I feel lighter than I have in days. Plus, I have to admit, it's nice to have my parents to myself for the evening. It's like I found a way to turn the calendar back to the night Dad and I sat at his computer and considered Camp Skylark. Only this time, instead of asking if I can decide later, I say yes, I'm going for it!

"So, Noodle," Dad says. "How far along are you in your summer reading?

I flush, having forgotten all about the three books I'm supposed to read before school starts. That's the only summer homework we get and, of course, it's my dad who assigns it.

"Um, not very," I admit.

"Well, you've got just over three weeks left. One book a week, Noodle."

I nod. I can probably finish a book this week, but after that, I'm leaving for Camp Skylark where I'll be busy all the time. Of course, I can't say that yet. Not until it's paid for, and they can't talk me out of it.

"She'll get it done," Mom assures him.

"I know she will," Dad agrees, and I start to feel terrible. They're both so trusting and nice to me. Eventually, I'm going to have to tell them everything. Not just that I'm going to camp after all, but why.

"I wonder how Alison is liking New York," Mom says, helping herself to some fried rice.

"She's probably having a great time," Dad answers. "I was

thinking we should take her to the city ourselves next weekend. She's dying to go to the Metropolitan Museum."

"Oh, let's," Mom says. "You'll love it, too, Mol."

A piece of broccoli lands like a rock in my stomach. I have to tell them. They'll still enjoy exploring the city without me, but they deserve to know that that's how it's going to be. "Um, Mom, Dad—"

But Dad interrupts me. "You know what else we need to make time for?" He points his chopsticks at me. "Another amusement park. One with a truly colossal roller coaster!"

"Really, Dad?" I glare at him, but he doesn't seem to notice, just like he didn't notice what a terrible time I had at Lessing's Cove.

Forget it, I think, shoving a hunk of chicken in my mouth. They already said yes to camp before. They can't take it back now. And, anyway, if Dad didn't want me to use his Pay-Buddy account, he shouldn't have picked my nickname as a password.

28

Didn't Dad make a rule for himself not to go on the computer after dinner?"

"Yes, he did," Mom agrees, but she doesn't seem too concerned about it. Curled up on the couch, she turns a page in her book and keeps reading.

I've finished the dishes, and now I need the study to myself for the few minutes it will take to pay for camp.

"What's he doing, anyway?"

"A friend invited him to play an online version of Scrabble. Can you stop pacing, Molly? I've read the same paragraph three times."

I sit on the arm of the couch, my mind racing. Maybe I can find the form on Mom's laptop. I'll just look for the Camp Skylark website and, if I need a password to log in, I'll try *Noodle* again.

"Mom, can I borrow your computer? There's a...a game Diane showed me I really like."

"Sorry, Mol. The battery's dead and I left the charger at work. How about starting one of your summer reading books?"

Sighing, I grab one off the pile and take Dad's usual place on the couch. I know I won't be able to concentrate, but I have to stop acting so weird, or Mom will get suspicious.

"'There is no friend as loyal as a book,'" she says, obviously quoting some writer.

I open the novel, but the words on the page are a blurry line of ants. *How long can Dad sit there playing Scrabble?* I want to ask, but I already know the answer. He can get hooked and stay all night, which is why he doesn't usually let himself go online in the evenings.

"I can't believe Alison didn't bring a laptop," I complain. "What twenty-year-old travels without a computer?"

"She's a rare girl," Mom says, finally looking up from the page. "You're not generally this computer-crazy, either. Must be a great game you played at Diane's."

"It is," I mumble.

I turn back to the book, hoping the story will make the time pass more quickly. But, though I follow the word ants across the page, the sentences they form make no sense to me. I rest my head back on the cushion and close my eyes.

Come on, Dad, hurry up. I think this as hard as I can without saying it aloud. *Come take my place on the couch, so I can do what I need to...*

After what feels like a minute, I hear a key in the lock.

I sit up, surprised to find the room dark and an afghan thrown over my legs.

"Mom?" I say, but I'm alone on the couch.

The door opens and the overhead light comes on, hurting my eyes.

"Sis? That you? Were you waiting up for me?"

Up in my room, Alison drops some shopping bags into the closet, and we both change into our nightgowns. Her sketchbook is in the pile right where I left it. It's an ordinary book with a plain beige cover, but as I sit on my bed, my eyes keep drifting toward it as though it glows.

"How did Laurel die?" I wonder. Alison, who's standing by the dresser, brushing her hair, stops in the middle of a stroke and stares at me through the mirror. That's when I realize I've spoken the question aloud.

After a moment, Alison asks, "Has your mum ever warned you not to rush out into the road from between parked cars?" She's talking to me, but watching her own reflection. "Well, it's good advice. Laurel was walking to school when she saw a group of our mates across the road. She ran to meet them and was hit by a lorry."

"A lorry?"

"A truck," Alison explains.

"Oh." The phrase *Laurel hit by a lorry* loops through my head like a sad nursery rhyme, like *Jack fell down and broke his crown*. "Were you there?"

"No, thank goodness." Alison's fingers go to her throat, and I see that she's wearing the chain from the heart necklace. "I would have been, but I was home that day with stomach cramps. Our mates were so shaken. Laurel was thrown in the air and came down hard enough that she died on the spot. There was nothing anyone could do."

Laurel hit by a lorry. My mind stays with the sounds of the words because I don't want to let pictures in to take their place. I also don't want to think about how easily that could happen to one of my friends. Or to me.

"Was this before I visited you in London?" I ask, though I already know the answer.

"About a year before." Alison comes to sit beside me on the bed. Her hair smells like a mix of melon and sweat.

"Why didn't you tell me? I remember you talking about your friend Laurel, but you never said she..." It's hard for me to finish the sentence, but Alison nods as though I did.

"For one thing, you were so little. But it was also my way of keeping her alive for myself, mentioning her when I could without saying the whole story." Her hand reaches for the chain again. "I shouldn't have gotten so mad at you about the necklace, but wearing it was another way I held her close. It's silly, but when I found out it broke, I felt like I lost her a second time."

"I don't think it's silly. Remember when I brought it home from London? I wanted to keep it as a way of having you with me, even though you live so far away."

Alison nods. "That was one powerful necklace," she says with a small laugh.

I know my next question might upset her, but I can't help asking.

"Alison? You seem so happy most of the time, but this terrible thing happened. If my good friend died, I think I'd be sad forever."

"I thought that too at first." She leans back against the wall. "But you know who helped me the most? Dad. For at least a month after Laurel died, I came home from school every day and closed myself in my room. Finally, my mum had Dad call me. First, he just listened to me cry. I'll never forget it. 'Let it out, sweetheart,' he kept saying. 'Let it out.' But then, later in the conversation, he said something that made me laugh."

"That sounds more like the dad I know," I say.

"Me, too. But I felt guilty for laughing and told him so. And he said, 'Alison, you didn't die. You have a life and you better start living it again. Promise me you'll at least take breaks from mourning now and then. See a movie. Let yourself laugh. I'm sure your friend would want that for you.'"

"Our dad said that?"

"He did. He may be a jester, but he can be wise too."

"And then you felt better?"

"Yeah. I took little breaks like he suggested. I went out with friends. I laughed at a joke on the telly. After a time, the breaks came naturally and lasted longer. I still get sad about Laurel, even now, but I don't stay sad for hours at a time. Something else that helped me was drawing. Here, I'll show you."

Alison gets off the bed, and I expect she'll grab the sketchbook from the dresser. Instead, she opens the chest where I keep my winter clothes and all her cards and notes. She pulls out a drawing pad and comes to sit beside me again.

Alison places the pad on my lap and begins turning the

pages. I recognize the girl in every picture as Laurel, though Alison has drawn her at all different ages. Of course, when we get to the end, she's only fourteen.

"Laurel's mum and dad let me come to their house as often as I liked to draw from their photographs. Eventually, I made them a painting from this one."

She flips back to a portrait of Laurel wearing pearl earrings and a lace blouse. "She was glammed up for her cousin's wedding."

"Her parents must have loved the painting."

"They did." Alison stares at the picture. "Laurel and I were actually just growing close in the last months of her life. I still miss her."

"I'm really sorry," I say, and I hope she knows I mean for everything. I'm sorry that Laurel died and that I broke Alison's one keepsake. And though she doesn't exactly know about this, I'm also sorry that, just because she seems to like Robbie Keller, I assumed she *was* like Robbie and lied to me.

"Oh, I've got something for you," Alison says. She goes back to the chest and begins to dig through it. A moment later, she's holding *The Sister Book*.

29

As relieved as I am that Alison didn't tear *The Sister Book* up and throw it away, I can't help but feel bad that she's returning it.

"This gift you made me is so special," she starts, still kneeling by the chest. At least she's going to be nice about it. She pulls out a package wrapped in tissue paper, then places *The Sister Book* back on top of my sweaters.

"What—" I say, confused.

"You inspired me to make something for you in return."

Alison places the package on my lap. It has the weight and shape of a small tray.

"You're giving me a gift? But I thought…" How should I finish the sentence? *I thought you hated me? I thought you'd be much happier if I wasn't here?*

It occurs to me that, other than the fact that Alison got angry when she first learned about the necklace, I'd made all our other problems up. It's like the time Mom spent a day believing Dad was mad at her, but she'd really just misunderstood his text.

"Open it," Alison urges.

I tear at the paper. Inside, I find a framed drawing: Alison and me, just as we look in the one old photograph of us together.

I stare and stare at it. Alison has captured her own shiny long hair and my messy pigtails. Our similarly shaped eyes and matching smiles. That unnamable something beneath the skin that somehow says we're closely related. You can even tell from my expression how much five-year-old me looked up to my sister.

"It's beautiful," I say, the image blurring as tears spring to my eyes.

Still, I'm confused by the fact that I saw Alison throw out *The Sister Book*. Did she change her mind at the last minute and dig it out of the trash? If I went and looked at it right now, would the pages be all taped and creased? Taking a breath, I stop the questions running through my head. *You should have just asked me*, I remember Dad saying to Mom after The Texting Incident.

"Alison? The other day, when you brought all that paper down to recycling—"

"Sketches for this drawing," she explains. "It took me a few tries to get it right."

"Oh," I say, biting back a smile. I look down, noticing the frame for the first time. It's made of smooth silver and has the word *Sisters* on it, the letters formed out of glittery beads.

"I bought that at the mall with your mum. Which reminds me…"

She pulls a shopping bag out from under the dresser and hands it to me. Inside is an empty frame just like the first. I look at Alison, unsure what this other one is for.

"We have to pester Dad to take our photograph so we can complete both our presents."

"You mean you'll do another drawing?"

"Righto," Alison answers.

I wonder if there will be enough time before I leave for Camp Skylark.

"To quote my sister, 'Place Picture Here,'" Alison says, and I remember I never completed the registration. I suppose I could stay. Maybe it's meant to be.

30

When I wake the next morning, Alison is sitting up in bed, studying a drawing. I crawl out of the covers and go sit beside her.

"Oh, that one," I say, flushing as I look over her shoulder. "It's supposed to be Diane, but I know it looks nothing like her. I'm just awful at faces."

"You did it from memory?" Alison asks.

"No. She was next to me while I sketched her."

"Here, show me." Alison hands me my pad. "Try to draw me."

"It'll look terrible," I warn her, but I grab a pencil and start drawing. I can't get the shape of the face right, or the eyes. The hair is okay, but even that could be more realistic.

"Here's the problem, sis. You're looking more at the page than at me. Let me show you."

Alison takes the pad, turns to a clean page, and starts to draw. "Now watch my eyes."

I do as she says, and what I see is that her eyes only flit to the page for brief seconds. The rest of the time, she's looking carefully at my face. Her concentration reminds me of someone watching the road as they drive.

"What you just did," she says, as she continues to draw, "was look at me for a couple of seconds, then glue your eyes to the paper and try to replicate what you saw."

She turns the page to face me, and the quick sketch looks remarkably like me.

"That's so good."

"Here. Try again. But this time, barely let your eyes drop to the page."

It takes some getting used to, but I force myself to keep my attention on Alison as I draw, only glancing at the paper long enough to be sure my pencil hasn't moved off the line. When I finish, it's not nearly as good as her sketch of me, but it does somehow capture her.

"Much better," she tells me.

I study my drawing and find the more I stare at it, the more I like it. It's so simple. Look at your subject as you work, not at the paper. The funny thing is, until Alison pointed it out, I hadn't realized I wasn't doing that all along.

Now, I'm more certain than ever that she should teach at my school.

"Alison," I say, surprised by how bold my voice sounds. "I think you should be an art teacher instead of a nanny. I know you liked being Roger Clark's student and all, but you did that already, and you're such a great artist."

"You want to see the work of a great artist?" she asks.

She goes to her pile of books, pulls out the biggest one, and sits beside me again to turn the glossy pages. I've never seen portraits like these. An old man on a beach chair, gazing at the sky. A child rubbing at a scab on his knee. A thin, tired-looking woman staring out a window. The backgrounds are painted so that you get a sense of what time of day it is and what the air feels like. What's even more amazing is that you not only know what kind of mood each person is in, but you can't help feeling their emotions along with them.

"These are beautiful," I tell Alison.

The last page names the museums where the paintings hang. And, on the back of the book, beneath a photograph of Roger Clark, is a list of all the awards he's won.

"Now do you see why I want to keep learning from him?"

I nod, though it still doesn't seem fair. We've never gotten to live together like sisters. Why couldn't she stay here? If she absolutely had to keep studying art, New York City isn't all that far to drive to, and I know some of the best painters in the world live there.

"Alison—" I start.

But before I can think of the right words, I hear a knock and look up to find Dad standing in the doorway. He's in his pajamas, and his hair is standing up at crazy angles.

"No interviews today?" I ask, hoping it still matters.

"Not one, thank goodness. I'm exhausted from that ridiculously addictive game."

We head downstairs, and Alison offers to make us omelets. Over breakfast, Dad asks her question after question about her time in the city. She describes interesting shops, an Indian restaurant with cloth-covered booths, a park filled with musicians and acrobats. I want to break in and mention all the art schools and galleries there, but they don't give me a chance.

"And the Keller boy?" Dad asks. "Did you enjoy being with him?"

I lean in, anxious to hear Alison's answer.

"Well…I think I'd rather go with you, Gail, and Molly next time."

"We were just talking about that last night," he tells her.

After we finish eating, Dad suggests a walk in the woods.

"Why don't you bring your camera, Dad?" Alison asks, winking at me.

"Good idea," I say, remembering our presents to each other.

Outside, the three of us walk quietly, listening to the birds and the rattle of leaves in the breeze. I think about the advice Dad gave Alison after Laurel died, to take breaks from her sadness and go live her life. Maybe it's time for me to take a break from worrying about how to get her to stay, and just enjoy being with my family. Besides, if Alison is supposed to live here—and in so many ways it seems like she is—she will. According to my mom, that's how *meant to be* works.

When we reach the clearing, Dad whips out his camera. Alison and I do a bunch of poses, some serious and some clowning around, all with our arms around each other.

Afterwards, we sit in the grass, knees touching, to choose the photo that she'll draw and I'll tape to the last page of *The Sister Book*. She holds the camera and clicks through each shot as I look on.

"How about this one?" she asks.

In the picture, the two of us lean against a tree stump. Her head is turned toward me, her smile an exact match of my own.

"Righto," I say to my sister.

31

I need a nap," Dad tells us when we come out of the woods. "No more nighttime computer games for me." As the back door slaps closed behind him, I turn to Alison. "So, I've been working on something else that I want you to see."

Taking my sister's hand, I lead her into the garage and up the back staircase. When we step into the attic, she gasps.

"It's an artist's garret," she exclaims. "Like in *La Bohème.*"

I'm not sure what she means, but I can tell she loves her new studio. She plops down on one of the cushions and looks around.

"Great light," she says. "Perfect for painting."

I grin so hard it almost hurts. Those are the same words she used to describe the room the Clarks set up for her.

"Diane found that easel when we were cleaning up in here," I tell her. "It's for you."

"Smashing. Shall we bring up some art supplies? We've got hours of good light left."

We. She said *we.* She wants us to do our art side by side, after all.

We slip into the house, closing the door quietly behind us so we don't wake Dad. Up in my room, Alison digs in the closet until she finds the box of paints she'd brought with her, along with a bag that says *NYC Paint and Paperie.* She motions for me to peek inside. Three clean canvases.

"I picked these up in Greenwich Village last night," she whispers. "Meant to be, eh?"

"Sure is," I say. This is falling into place so perfectly, it almost seems magical.

I grab a pad, some pencils, and a photo of Diane, so I can practice my new drawing technique and surprise her.

Up in the attic, we play the radio softly. Alison stands at the easel, directly under the skylight, painting with that same look of concentration I'd seen on her face while she drew my picture this morning. I sit cross-legged on a cushion and practice keeping my eyes on the photo I'm working from. As I stare at my best friend's oh-so-familiar face, I remember how, yesterday, she sat right here and cried over all the keepsakes my parents saved from my life. I also think about the fact that her dad's absence has always seemed normal to me. It strikes me that there are all kinds of normal and all kinds of families.

Alison steps back from her painting and gazes at it, tapping her mouth with the wooden end of her brush. I can't help laughing when I notice I'm doing the same thing right now with my pencil. She turns and smiles at me, and I feel flooded with love for my sister. I realize with a start that I don't want to take her away from studying with Roger Clark. After all, he's such an important painter, and she's really excited about it.

"Alison," I say, breaking a code between artists by interrupting her.

She must be ready for a break because she lays down her brush and comes to sit beside me.

"Are the Clarks home with their kids right now?" I hear myself ask.

"They are. They're both professors, so they have the summers off."

"Then you will, too, once you start working for them?"

"That's right. Nice, eh?"

"So…" I scoot over so that I'm pressed right up against my sister, breathing in her melon-scented hair. "I think we should make this a regular thing. You should come stay here every August."

For a moment, Alison is quiet, considering.

Having her here once a year for a month is very different from having her here all the time, but somehow it feels right.

"You know, sis," she says, draping her arm around my shoulder, "I'd love that."

All kinds of normal and all kinds of families. The more I think about this, the more I realize how true it is. Diane's dad doesn't live with them. One of our friends at school has two moms, and another is being raised by her grandparents. I may be the only kid I know whose sibling doesn't live with her full-time, but even that's about to change with Robbie leaving for college in September. He'll be back by the time Alison comes again next August, but it doesn't sound like she's interested in spending any more time with him.

Even though my sister won't always be here like I'd hoped, I still feel pleased with our plan. Dad loves the idea, too, though he didn't love that we slammed into the house and woke him up to tell him about it.

While we were talking, the phone rang. From Dad's side of the conversation, I knew it was someone from the search committee describing the new resumes they received.

"Now that one has possibilities," I heard Dad say. "Can we meet her tomorrow?"

He grabbed a notepad and scribbled something down, then asked a few more questions. For the first time since we learned about Mrs. Lamb going to another school, I felt glad the committee was working so hard to find a good replacement.

Now, back in the attic, Alison has returned to her painting, and I focus on my own project. I've put aside the drawing I'd started so I can sew sheets of cream-colored stationary together and make a book.

Tonight, while my parents sit reading, and my sister chats with her mum on the webcam, I'll gather pictures of Diane and me. We may not be related, but to me we're family. And since no one has ever put together a photo album or a baby book for her, I've decided to present her with a *Sister Book* of her own. The first page will hold a snapshot from when we were babies crawling after each other in one of our back-yards, and the last will be a blank that says, "Place Picture Here." For that, we'll have someone take our photo in our artist garret. Maybe only the two of us will pose, or maybe we'll include Carly and Alison. It's Diane's *Sister Book*, so I'll leave that for her to decide.

ACKNOWLEDGMENTS

Writing may be a solitary endeavor, but, thank goodness, no book is born in a vacuum.

Heartfelt thanks to Suzanne Kamata, Caren Lissner, and Julia Hough who read early versions of this manuscript, and gave me kind and invaluable feedback. I also want to thank Julia for all she's taught me through the years about friendship and chosen sisterhood.

Special thanks to Amy Fuchs-Zuelch for making a place in her loving, raucous home for this almost-only child back when I needed it most.

Gratitude beyond words to Jaynie Royal and Pam Van Dyk, the amazing women of Regal House Publishing and Fitzroy Books. Their warmth, their faith in this book, and their genius at bringing literature into the world and building community has blown me away and buoyed me through every part of the process. Thanks, too, to the writers of Regal House who have welcomed me into the fold—Gabriel Arquilevich, Carol Dines, Cliff Garstang, Sandra Waugh, Melanie Downing, my old friend Zack Rogow, and my new Fitzroy sister Kimberly Kenna. Finding the right home for a book is always a joy, but I never imagined it could come with a family.

And speaking of family, unending love and gratitude to my husband Daniel Simpson for listening to this book countless times, preventing me from sending Molly out into chapter fifteen on an empty stomach, and devoting an entire afternoon to helping me put all my commas in the right place. Anyone who says two writers living together is a bad idea clearly never had the privilege of living with him.

Thanks, also, to my niece Naomi Ages—daughter, sister, friend, all in one beautiful package. And finally, deepest love and gratitude to my son Ethan Gilbert for being his brilliant, hilarious, loving self and for reminding me to live not just on the page, but in the world.

Book Club Questions

1) Why does Molly make The Sister Book for Alison? What does she hope it will help Alison to understand?

2) Why do you think it's so important to Molly that Alison come live with her and her parents? Is there anything about the shape of your family, or your day-to-day life together, that you wish you could change?

3) When Alison gives Molly an art lesson, she tells her to look at the person she's drawing as much as possible as she works, rather than focusing on her own hand on the page. Are there ways this advice could be helpful to Molly that have nothing to do with drawing? How?

4) How are Molly and Diane like sisters to each other? Is there someone you're not related to who feels like a part of your family? If so, what is it about your relationship that makes you feel that way? If not, how are your relationships with family members unlike those with close friends?

5) At the end of the story, Molly realizes that there are all kinds of normal and all kinds of families. What does this mean?